*A Harlequin Romance*

OTHER

## *Harlequin Romances*

by MARY BURCHELL

1029—CHOOSE WHICH YOU WILL
1075—CINDERELLA AFTER MIDNIGHT
1100—THE BROKEN WING
1117—DEARLY BELOVED
1138—LOVING IS GIVING
1165—WARD OF LUCIFER
1187—SWEET ADVENTURE
1214—THE MARSHALL FAMILY
1244—WHEN LOVE IS BLIND
1270—THOUGH WORLDS APART
1298—MISSING FROM HOME
1330—A HOME FOR JOY
1354—WHEN LOVE'S BEGINNING
1382—TO JOURNEY TOGETHER
1405—THE CURTAIN RISES
1431—THE OTHER LINDING GIRL
1455—GIRL WITH A CHALLENGE
1474—MY SISTER CELIA
1508—CHILD OF MUSIC
1543—BUT NOT FOR ME
1567—DO NOT GO, MY LOVE
1587—MUSIC OF THE HEART

# ONE MAN'S HEART

by

MARY BURCHELL

HARLEQUIN BOOKS

TORONTO
WINNIPEG

Original hard cover edition published
by Mills & Boon Limited, 17 - 19 Foley Street
London W1A 1DR, England

Harlequin edition published October, 1972


SBN 373-01632-8

*All the characters in this book have no existence outside the imagination of the Author, and have no relation whatsoever to anyone bearing the same name or names. They are not even distantly inspired by any individual known or unknown to the Author, and all the incidents are pure invention.*



Printed in Canada

1632

## CHAPTER ONE

HILMA drew the hood of her velvet cape over her head with entirely steady fingers. It was no use embarking on an adventure of this sort with anything but good nerves. Difficult, of course, to imagine that the "adventure" was nothing less than robbing a flat. But—Hilma gave the faintest sigh of regret—necessity was the mother of a lot of things besides invention.

This was one of the things.

Letting herself out of the silent house, she walked resolutely to the nearby taxi rank.

Two or three drivers, engaged in amiably ferocious discussion, were propped up against the railings. But the moment Hilma put her hand on the door of the first taxi, a fat, heavily-breathing driver detached himself from the group, with the final dictum, "Nuts! That's what you are—nuts!" and came towards her. "Yes, ma'am?"

"Do you know the Glaudia Cinema?" She gave him the slight, casual smile which usually made all porters, taxi-drivers and male shop assistants jump to do her bidding.

"Big new place on a corner, just out of Oxford Street, isn't it?"

"Yes, that's it."

"Bit late for the performance, aren't you, miss?" The different form of address testified to the effectiveness of Hilma's smile, and he gave a hoarse, rather bronchial chuckle as he held the door open for her.

"It would be, certainly. I'm meeting someone there after the show."

He didn't say, "*Your* evening's just beginning, I suppose." He simply said "Ah!"—but with a world of meaning, and gave her a benevolent look as he shut the door and climbed slowly into the driving seat.

The taxi turned westward, and Hilma's thoughts ran on ahead of her.

She had timed it very well. With anything like luck she should arrive just as the crowd from that big charity première were streaming out. There should be no difficulty whatever in going in at one door and out at another—the one at the back of the theatre which led almost immediately into the darker, unfrequented streets beyond the immediate fringe of London's night life.

The taxi drew up with a jerk.

"Here y'are, miss. Just in time. He won't have had no anxious minutes. You'll just catch him." And the driver chuckled again at his own wit as he pocketed his fare and jerked his head in the direction of the stream of well-dressed people who were beginning to issue from the ornate entrance of the Glaudia.

It was even easier than she had imagined. Making her way through the crowded foyer, she pretended to be looking for someone. A short pause by the farther exit would have indicated to even the closest observer that she had missed whoever she was seeking, and, with the faintest shrug, she turned away to the left, walking purposefully but with no special air of hurry. A few minutes later she had become just any one of London's theatregoers, walking home on a clear, dark night. The long dark cloak with the enveloping hood wiped out identity in a very satisfactory way.

Lucky that Charles should have elected to live in

one of the few blocks of flats where there was an outside fire-escape. Almost like Providence—except that Hilma found it difficult to suppose Providence had much to do with this little escapade—that he should once have said something about his flat looking straight on to the fire-escape.

She supposed she ought to feel much more frightened than she did. But then there was something in the saying that fortune favoured the brave. It wasn't really fortune, of course, but just that those who kept cool and clear-thinking could work everything out to the *n*th degree and profit by every chance as it came along.

Even Hilma had to admit, however, that it was sheer good luck when she discovered that the one street lamp which might have proved dangerous had, for some reason, gone out. The narrow mews which ran along the back of the block were in almost complete darkness.

Perhaps, she thought grimly, this was more a case of the devil looking after his own than fortune favouring the brave. It didn't really matter. The result was equally desirable, whatever the cause.

The only thing to make sure of now was that she got the number of the floor right. Five hundred and eleven—that was the number of Charles's flat, and the notice in the entry, where she had looked a few days ago, stated quite plainly that "the 'hundred' number indicates the floor on which the flat is situated."

Standing in a deep patch of shadow, she slowly counted up the floors. Her heart rose uncomfortably in her throat as she saw that light was streaming from one window. Then she realised that, even in this, her incredible luck had held. The lighted window was one floor above Charles's. She would not have to pass it.

It even served to throw the floor immediately below it into deeper shadow.

With an agility born of her slenderness, as well as schoolday escapades shared with an adventurous brother, she scaled the wall which shut off the flats from the mews. There was a horrid moment when she felt that, shadow or no shadow, she must surely be outlined against the night sky. Then she was hanging by her slim, strong hands from the top of the wall, feeling for even the slightest foothold.

There was none, and, after a breathless moment of indecision, she risked the drop. As she landed she realised that she had touched the crowning point of her good luck. By a matter of less than six inches she had missed a line of dustbins.

Even so, the nearness of the disaster shook her badly, and for a moment she leant against the wall, her heart beating uncomfortably hard.

There was nothing to be afraid of now. The iron fire-escape was just beside her, winding up and up into the darkness. Silently she took out the penknife she had with her and opened it. Even then, the very feel of it made her smile. It was Tony's school penknife, and this was not the first time it had been used to slip back the catch of a window. More than one moonlight outing, when they stayed on their grandfather's farm as children, had ended in a stealthy return by way of the kitchen window.

She hoped her hand had not lost its cunning—that was all.

Silent as a shadow herself, she climbed upwards.

Blessings on the lighted window! It marked the position of the floor so well. The was no fear of miscounting the turns in the stairs and arriving at the wrong floor.

Hilma was breathless by the time she had reached

the right floor, and as she leant there in the comparative safety of the window embrasure, she found that her hand was shaking in a way that made it rather difficult to slip the penknife between the two sashes of the window.

It was done at last, however, and with a slight but terrifying sound the catch clicked back.

It didn't really matter about the sound, of course. There was no question whatever about Charles being away for the whole week-end, but when one's nerves were taut even the least sound seemed to twang on them as though they were tight wires.

Very slowly—the blood pressed back painfully from her finger-tips with the effort—Hilma raised the window. The hand which she stretched out in front of her came against thick velvet curtains. The next moment she had slipped over the sill into the room, softly lowered the window, and pushed aside the curtains.

It was a strange and frightening sensation, going forward into that pit of velvet darkness. Turning, she pulled the curtains close behind her and switched on the little electric torch she had in her pocket.

There was something reassuring about that pencil of light that fell across the carpet—something even more reassuring about the realisation that she *had* surmounted every obstacle. She was here in Charles's sitting-room, alone in the flat, with hours—the whole week-end, if she liked—in front of her. She couldn't possibly fail to find that wretched letter. She would go about it boldly and systematically.

With admirable coolness she examined the curtains, ascertained that they must shut out every glimmer of light from the outside, and then crossed over and switched on the electric light.

That was better. She could see the whole room now. She looked round almost critically.

Rather different from the flat *she* used to know. More masculine—less pseudo-artistic. But then Charles was probably running some new pose by now. It was quite immaterial in any case. The only important thing was that the writing bureau in the corner was the place where a man would keep his letters.

Hilma went over and tried it. She was almost glad to find it locked. That meant he kept things there which he valued. Letters from silly women, for instance. Letters that could, in certain circumstances, realise quite a lot of money.

With the boldness of previous success, she slipped Tony's penknife under the lock, and exerted all her strength. This time the sound of splintering wood was a good deal louder than the snap of any window-catch, but it hardly disturbed her. She felt sure success was almost within her grasp.

Hilma lifted back the flap of the bureau and bent eagerly over the confusion of papers inside.

Compromising letters would hardly be among that haphazard pile. Rather they would be tucked away in the pigeonholes at the back. Her hand was actually on the first roll of papers when a voice spoke almost casually behind her.

"I hate to disturb anyone so deeply occupied. But do you mind telling me what you are doing?"

For a moment Hilma was so terrified that she could not bring herself to turn round. Then she swung round abruptly, her hands spread out either side of her against the bureau.

The man who was regarding her was tall and dark and not a little grim. He leant against the side of the doorway, one hand thrust into the pocket of his smoking-jacket, and his eyes were slightly narrowed as they watched her.

Hilma made a desperate attempt to think quickly and coolly. *What* was he doing there?—There was only one possible explanation. Charles had lent this friend of his the flat for the week-end. She must bluff. Quickly, quickly! But what to say?

It was really only a matter of seconds before her answer came, and it was wonderfully, incredibly cool.

"What a terrible start you gave me! And what are *you* doing, might I ask? Mr. Martin happened to lend me this flat for the week-end."

"So?" He didn't seem enormously impressed by the statement, and, coming a step or two into the room, he carelessly bent and picked up the penknife which she had let fall on the floor. "And you return the favour by opening his bureau?"

Another horrible moment—but she surmounted it with a brazen little laugh.

"All right, I'll own to the most ghastly curiosity about something in that desk. It's a feminine vice, you know, and I don't know that I'm prepared to accept your condemnation of it."

He considered that, balancing the knife thoughtfully on the palm of his hand.

"You know Mr. Martin very well, of course?"

"Oh, yes." She gave a much more casual little laugh that time. "I've known him for years."

"And often visited him here?"

There was only a second's hesitation. But if she claimed sufficient familiarity with him to borrow his flat it would be hopeless to say "No" to that question.

"Why, certainly." She even infused considerable surprise into that, and a delicate intimation that she was finding this catechism impertinent and unnecessary "But——"

"You were"--he glanced reflectively at the window—"you were unconventional enough to arrive by the window?" he suggested politely.

Again Hilma hesitated a moment for an answer, and he seemed to take her silence for agreement.

"It's a novel idea, certainly—very novel." Those disturbingly penetrating eyes came back to her face. " But in future, young lady, I advise you to use the door. It may be dull, but at least it ensures that you get the number right."

"The—number?" Hilma's eyes widened until their startling blue was almost swallowed up in the blackness of her pupils. She didn't know that the man regarding her thought she made a wonderful picture, with the dark velvet hood falling back from her corn-coloured hair, and her face very white except for the red, parted lips.

"Exactly. The number," he agreed pleasantly. "Now suppose you wash out the rest of the invention and tell me just why you were rifling *my* desk. The other story was good for a speedy invention, but it had a lot of holes in it, you know."

Hilma was not quite sure whether he made an ironically hospitable gesture towards the arm-chair, but in any case she sank into it. For one thing she was incapable of standing any longer when her knees felt so unsteady.

He seemed quite willing to let her take her time, but she thought, as he lounged against the table, he showed every expectation of getting his answer eventually.

"Your knife." He leant forward and politely returned it to her, but when she curled her fingers nervously over it he quite calmly took her hands in his and gently unclasped them. "No, don't do that. You'll hurt yourself. There's no need to register terror, you know. You're much too lovely to be really afraid of a mere man. Besides"—he smiled, and the smile even touched his eyes—"surely young women who find the courage to break in via the fire-escape are brave enough to tackle awkward explanations."

She glanced at him then and recovered a little of her nerve.

"I don't think," she said coolly, "that I feel inclined to make explanations to *you*."

"And I think," he retorted with a hint of that dangerous pleasantness again, "I think that you'd better."

"Better?" She gave a proud little lift of her chin. "Better! Why, pray?"

"Because," he told her carelessly, "if you refuse, I shall give you five minutes to come to a wiser decision and then I shall send for the police."

"The—police!" She went very white again. "You *couldn't*!"

"Why not?"

"Because——" She made a helpless little gesture that he found more pathetic than his expression suggested. "Oh, it's not a reason. Only you sounded more lenient, more—human, just now when you spoke about—about my being beautiful."

He laughed then, with real amusement, but he shook his head.

"Oh, no. I'm sorry to disappoint you, but that counts more against you than for you."

"I don't understand."

"Don't you?" His dark eyes travelled over her with an open appreciation that was entirely inoffensive. "Well, you're quite lovely enough to confuse any issue, so I shall be brutally suspicious in order to be on the safe side."

Against her will, that appealed to her sense of humour. She smiled faintly, but almost immediately spoke very earnestly again.

"I *did* make an honest mistake. I thought this was Charles Martin's flat."

"After having visited it so often?" He studied the pattern of the carpet with a reflective smile.

"Oh!" She flushed deeply, which played havoc with her little air of sophistication. "I'm sorry. You—you win there. That was a lie."

"You are not, I hope, expecting me to believe that all the rest was the truth?" he murmured deprecatingly, rather as though he hated to call her a liar to her face—but there it was.

That did nothing to reduce the flush and, with a nervous gesture, she pushed back her fair hair. It fell over her forehead again in a heavy wave, and the man watched all the time with a curious degree of interest.

"Before anything else," she stated firmly, "I'm going to ask *you* a question."

"We-ell, I don't want to seem discourteous, but you are not really very well placed for that. Not to put too fine a point on it, *I* am the one to decide who shall ask the questions. However, what is it you want to ask?"

"Do you know Mr. Martin at all?"

"Only by sight, and sufficiently to be aware that he occupies the flat immediately above this one."

"*Above* this one!" She thought confusedly of the lighted window and of the number of floors which she had counted so carefully. "Really, I don't understand," Hilma murmured half to herself.

"What don't you understand?"

"I thought," she quoted wearily, "the 'hundreds' number indicates the floor on which the flat is situated."

He gave her a glance of curious amusement.

"The truth is—you don't know this block of flats at all, do you?"

"Well—no, I don't. Mr. Martin lived somewhere else when—when I knew him."

"So that you couldn't be aware that the flats on the ground floor have a nought for the 'hundred' number."

"*Oh!*"

"Too bad," he agreed with mocking sympathy.

But she was hardly listening to him.

"That explains about the number," she said slowly. "But not about the light."

"The light?"

"There's a light blazing away from the window of Ch—of Mr. Martin's window. And yet I *know* he was away for the week-end."

He refused to share her bewilderment.

"But if it transpired that he was not"—again his air was grave, but there was an undercurrent of laughter in his voice—"that wouldn't be your only miscalculation, would it?"

It was absurd, but once more, in spite of all the chagrin and anxiety, her sense of humour forced a reluctant smile.

"Pretty badly bungled all along, wasn't it?" she said.

"I'm afraid so." They looked at each other—that curious current of sympathetic amusement running between them. Then he said patiently, "Let's go back to the beginning, shall we?"

"Hm. Or else you send for the police?"

"Don't make me repeat such a horrid statement," he begged.

"Well then, I'll explain." She paused, as though to collect her thoughts, and he watched her with an air of grave attention which she found oddly attractive. "I think," she said slowly, "that you must be a man of the world——"

He made her a slight bow.

"And so you'll know that—that there are times when a woman can do very foolish things."

"Even a very lovely woman?"

"Oh, yes. In fact, she's even more apt to do so than the other kind."

"Of course," he agreed gravely. "There is more ——"

"Temptation."

"I was going to say 'opportunity,' " he assured her.

"Very well, it's the same thing. Usually it happens when one is very young."

He began to laugh.

"What is there amusing in that?" she wanted to know.

"My dear, are we still talking about you?"

"Of course. Why not?"

"Only that it's delicious to hear you talking of your vanished youth."

"Oh!" She laughed a little too, then. "Well, I was twenty when it happened."

"So?" The dark eyes travelled over her again with such frank curiosity as well as admiration that she said, rather dryly:

"Twenty-five."

"Oh—thank you." Again he made her that half-mocking little bow. "And when you were twenty you—you committed a grave indiscretion?"

"Well, at least, I was preparing to do so. Spend a week-end with a man, you know."

He nodded regretfully. It seemed he did know.

"I went, but—well, I changed my mind—came back in time, you understand."

"Perfectly. Most discreetly expressed—and very wise of you, if I may say so."

"Yes, but the *un*wise part was that I had written a letter—quite an unmistakable letter—making the arrangement."

"And that did *not* come back," he suggested.

"Exactly."

"The gentleman in the case—we will call him Mr. Martin, for the sake of argument, shall we?"

"Purely for the sake of argument," she agreed, a curious little dimple making its appearance in the centre of her cheek.

"The gentleman in the case preserved the letter carefully and produced it at a very awkward moment?"

"Threatened do produce it," she amended.

"Oh—threatened, of course. I'm a little unfamiliar with the technique, I'm afraid." His eyes sparkled, and then he enquired bluntly: "What made the moment specially awkward?"

"The usual reason." Her tone was a trifle dry. "I'm engaged—going to be married very soon."

"I see." He glanced at her ringless hand, and her eyes followed his.

"No," she said. "No, I didn't wear it tonight. It's rather a big diamond and——"

"You found difficulty in getting your burglar's glove over it?" he suggested.

"Not at all. As you see, I'm wearing no gloves." She spread out rather strong white hands for his inspection. "The fact is"—her tone was as grave as his, though that dimple appeared again—"that I thought the flash of it would betray my presence on the fire-escape."

"Whew—does he like them as large and imposing as all that?"

"Pretty nearly." There was a curious dryness in her tone again.

"But these generous views don't extend to—letters, shall we say?"

"No," Hilma agreed. "No, they do not."

"So that it became imperative to retrieve that unfortunate letter?"

"Yes—absolutely imperative. And"—the shadow of very real anxiety darkened her eyes again—"and I haven't got it, after all."

His eyes narrowed slightly as they had when he had watched her at the desk. But she was looking away from him, silent and troubled, and she failed to see the quick play of expression on his strong, good-looking face.

"We must make other plans, in fact," he remarked thoughtfully at last.

"We?" She flashed a glance at him then.

"We," he agreed, and smiled straight at her.

"Oh!" Something about that seemed to break her control badly for a moment. Her mouth quivered uncontrollably and she looked down. "I don't know why you should trust my story, or be so—so nice." She put out her hand to him, her head still bent, and immediately long, strong, brown fingers closed over hers.

He didn't say anything, but the clasp of their hands was curiously eloquent.

"I think," she said, looking up at him with an unsteady little smile, "I think you must be a born romantic."

"Not at all," he assured her earnestly. "Actually, I'm a distinctly selfish realist. Most people would call me an opportunist, I suppose."

"Then they would be wrong."

"No." He was regretful but firm. " I wish I could agree with you. But I can't. Almost my only positive virtue is an inability to hide the truth from myself. That tells me I'm the kind of man who deliberately sets out to make a rich marriage, for instance."

It was she who studied him with frank curiosity that time.

"And have you had any—any success?" she enquired delicately.

He nodded.

"I, too, am engaged," he admitted, and his degree of enthusiasm accurately balanced hers when speaking of her fiancé.

"Is she—nice?"

"Certainly."

"And very rich?"

"And very rich," he agreed.

"Oh, dear!" Hilma gave a slight sigh. "We're not very admirable people, are we?"

"Not very. Possibly that's why we feel instinctively drawn towards each other."

"Do we?" She felt she must not let that pass without challenge.

"Of course." He was unabashed. "The attraction even went to the lenghts of bringing you in at the wrong window."

She laughed, and he said calmly:

"Will you stay and have supper with me?"

"But I—there's still the letter."

"Of course. But didn't you say there was a light in the window above this?"

"Yes." She frowned again. "I can't understand it."

"Well, I'll tell you something. He goes out very often late at night, this—blackmailer friend of yours. He's home at the moment, in spite of all your calculations. But if you will honour me by taking supper with me, that will give him time to go out to his usual midnight haunts."

"But how shall we be sure that the coast is clear?"

"We shall look out and see if the light is gone, of course, and if it has I shall telephone to his flat. Anyone can make a mistake in a telephone number. If he answers—I've made a mistake in the number, and we must try something else, perhaps some other night. If there's no answer—the coast is clear."

Hilma nodded.

"We could look out now to see if the light is gone," she suggested.

"My dear, that's really horrid of you," he said, "and not at all in keeping with the spirit of romantic adventure which has fallen on us both."

She laughed and coloured slightly, whereat he took both her hands and drew her gently to her feet.

"How does this unfasten?" He bent to examine the clasp of her cloak.

"I haven't said I shall stay," she protested. But he was already unfastening the clasp, and at the second's light touch of his fingers on her throat she felt the protest die.

It was impossible to tell from his grave dark eyes whether he even noticed the moment, but to Hilma it administered the strangest little shock. Half puzzling, half frightening—wholly delicious.

"There." He stood before her now, the velvet cloak

over his arm. "Will you come in to supper? It's in the other room."

"We're—we're alone in the flat, of course?" The slight lift of her eyebrows emphasised the lateness of the hour and the curious unconventionality of what they were doing.

"Of course."

The last vestige of doubt seemed to drop from her then.

"Can I help get supper ready?" she volunteered.

"No. My man set it all out before he left."

"You have your own manservant?"

"Yes."

"Isn't that pretty expensive?"

"Yes. But so are most things worth having."

"I suppose they are." She was silent for a moment, then added slowly, "I suppose we *are* right in thinking that?"

"Well"—his smile was something between cynicism and indulgence—"are you prepared to face the rest of life without much money?"

"No," Hilma admitted. "No, I can't say I am."

"Hence the fiancé with a lavish taste in diamonds but a meagre supply of tolerance."

"I'm afraid," Hilma said, "that I don't really approve of your strange aptitude for approximating to the truth."

He laughed softly.

"You know, the trouble is that we're a little too much alike in outlook not to read each other's motives rather easily."

She made a slight face.

"Isn't that a slightly uncomfortable suggestion? Let's go in to supper."

He held the door open for her, but just as she was

about to pass him, she stopped and said with a worried little frown:

"He's really an awfully good sort, you know. Probably much too good for me."

"I'm sure she's much too good for me, too," he agreed with that mocking gravity. And then they went into the charming, candle-lit dining-room together.

He brought extra china, glass and silver for her and set it out deliberately. She stood watching him and thinking how well he did himself in everything. In style and choice this was the meal of a pretty extravagant person. Not too lavish, but undeniably exclusive.

When they were seated, he poured out wine for them both—clear amber-coloured wine from Italy, which seemed to have brought with it something of the warm, romantic inconsequence of the sunlit slopes where it had been made.

He raised his glass and silently toasted her, his smiling eyes never leaving her face.

Hilma thought there must be something very heady about this wine, for, as she drank, it seemed to her that a warm, delicious recklessness took hold of her. But her voice was quite cool as she said:

"Why do you look at me like that?"

"I'm trying to decide what to call you."

She raised her eyebrows.

"You mean you want to know my name?"

But he shook his head.

"No, no. Discretion and romance are at one on that. Throughout this delightful, brief adventure we can be only one thing—nameless."

"I suppose you're right," Hilma agreed slowly.

"But I know what I shall call you," he said softly. "What I'm sure my Austrian grandfather would have called you if he'd known you."

"And that is?"

"Liebling."

She coloured faintly again, perhaps at the peculiarly caressing quality of his voice when he said the word.

"That means—darling, doesn't it?"

"It is perhaps a little softer—a little gentler than darling." There was a strange quality of sweetness about his smile as he said that.

"That's very—nice of you. Almost too nice."

"Nothing could be too nice for this evening—Liebling."

She hardly knew what to reply. For one thing she was so startlingly in agreement with that view herself. After a moment she said, quite casually:

"So you had an Austrian grandfather?"

"Yes. Viennese."

"I—see. You know Vienna very well?"

"I did. In the old days."

"I think I'm not very much surprised to hear that. There's something a little Viennese about your charm." He inclined his head to her in amused acknowledgment of the compliment. "It's appropriate to—to our adventure somehow, too," she added, thoughtfully turning her glass on its stem.

"I wonder why you say that." His eyes were curiously gentle as they watched her.

"Because, in spite of the surface gaiety, there is an undercurrent of melancholy in everything Viennese."

"Melancholy, Liebling?"

"No. Perhaps that's too strong a word. I once heard someone say that Schubert's music expresses it exactly. It's a beauty like the spring. We all love it with an added tenderness because we feel instinctively that it can't last long."

There was a moment of profound silence. Then he said softly:

"So that's how you feel about our meeting, Liebling? You love it with an added tenderness because you know it can't last long?"

"Oh!" She looked up quickly and flushed. "I didn't mean quite——"

"Yes, you did, my dear. And you were right. This is our short and lovely and faintly melancholy moment. On either side of it lie our prosaic lives. We came from them. We shall go back to them, because necessity and our own rather selfish characters are something we cannot or will not fight against. But don't let's tarnish the moment by refusing to admit its brightness."

She smiled at him then and unhesitatingly raised her glass.

"To our moment," she said, and drank with her eyes on his.

There was a short silence after that while they began to eat the kind of meal that Hilma very seldom saw nowadays. She experienced a cool, almost impersonal appreciation of it. Not so much the physical enjoyment of eating good things as the satisfaction that such things existed and that all life had not narrowed down to the drab, commonplace of daily existence.

After a while he said smilingly:

"There are so many questions that I've presumed to ask you, Liebling. Aren't there any that you want to ask me?"

It amused her faintly, and for some reason touched her too, that he made this oddly ingenuous attempt to stir her curiosity in him. It was like a child who says, "Look at me, look at me. Don't you think I've climbed up high?" And that there should be anything childlike in the make-up of this big, dark, imperturbable stranger was piquant.

"I thought we were to remain very mysterious and anonymous," she said juste a little teasingly.

"Oh—yes. But there are some questions one can ask, and even answer, without casting too glaring a searchlight upon our identities."

"Very well, then there *is* something I feel very curious about."

"Yes?" He leant his elbows on the table and smiled straight at her.

"Tell me, is there any—any *explanation* of your wanting so passionately to have the good things of life?—or is it just——"

"A weakness of character?" he suggested.

She nodded.

"By 'explanation' you mean 'excuse,' of course?"

"I suppose I do."

"Well, there's no excuse, Liebling. There never is for being a dilettante instead of an honest-to-God fighter. What one might consider something of a reason is that all my life I've been used to the good things, that I never imagined that pleasant state of affairs altering, and now—or rather, a few months ago—instead of inheriting what I had expected, I find that someone else has been more fortunate than I."

"Oh! That's too bad," she exclaimed indignantly.

"Except that I suppose a man is at liberty to leave his money where he pleases."

"It was your father who did that?"

"My grandfather."

"Not the Austrian grandfather?"

"Oh, no. He had nothing much to leave—except his temperament."

"And he left you that?" Her blue eyes were almost tender suddenly.

"I don't know, Liebling." He smiled and shrugged. "You were kind enough to hint something of the sort a little while ago."

She nodded, perhaps in confirmation of that.

"So that, having been used to lots of money all your life, you suddenly find yourself more or less without any?"

"The unhappy truth in a nutshell," he agreed.

"I think that's an excuse," she exclaimed indignantly, "a very good excuse for deliberately setting out to—to acquire the good things of life again."

He seemed amused by her championship, but he slightly shook his head.

"No, no. A really admirable character would put up a fight, you know. Accept the circumstances, start at the bottom of the ladder—or whatever the uncomfortable expression is—and carve out his own fortune in the face of all obstacles."

"And you don't feel like doing that?"

"Not at all, Liebling. I happen to be a lazy man with expensive tastes, and so——"

"You make a very wealthy marriage?"

"Exactly."

"You said she was nice, I think. Do you—do you like her?"

"Since identities are not being disclosed, I can tell you that 'like' is exactly the word."

"You don't—love her?"

"Liebling, do you really expect me to sit in front of anyone as lovely as you and say I love another woman?" he demanded mockingly.

"Please—I'm serious."

"We ought not to be that, you know—serious. It doesn't fit in with the mood at all. But—since you insist on a reply—I love her about as much as you love the man whose ring you're not wearing."

"Oh!" Hilma's right hand went instinctively to cover her ringless left hand.

"Well, you don't love him, do you?" His smiling eyes challenged her.

"Do you expect me to sit in front of anyone as handsome as you——" she began mockingly in her turn, but he interrupted her quite urgently with:

"Seriously, Liebling."

"Very well." She spoke seriously and slowly. "Very well, I like him."

"Ah!" He presumed to give a little sigh of relief. "You have lifted a weight from my mind."

"That doesn't really mean anything at all, of course," she said severely.

"Doesn't it?" he laughed. "Don't you think it would have meant the ruin of our romantic meeting if you had started to tell me how much you loved someone else."

"You know"—she looked at him gravely—"you're much more shameless about it all than I am. And yet I thought I was hard enough."

"Did you? How dare you think anything so harsh of yourself?" And then, as though to offset the tenderness of that: "So you're marrying for money, too?"

"Yes." There was a faintly defiant note in her voice.

"Any explanations?" he wanted to know. "Any excuses, Liebling?"

"Yes," she said slowly, "*I* think it's an excuse. You see, I do know the kind of life you're determined not to sample. I know everything there is to know about keeping up appearances on next to nothing, being gradually dropped by all the friends who do the only things one is interested in, watching the pleasant, casual things of family life becoming embittered and gradually crumbling under the strain of bills, bills,

bills and no money to meet them. After seeing what I've seen, I wouldn't marry a poor man if he looked like the Angel Gabriel and had the disposition of a saint."

"It would be a very, very boring combination in any case," her companion assured her. "And almost impossible to live up to."

Hilma gave a cross little laugh.

"You think it's all rather amusing, anyway, don't you?"

"No, my dear." He was quite serious. "I don't think it's amusing. I think it's very sad. After all, you have actually experienced all this. I've done nothing but regard the shadow of it and retreat determinedly."

"Well, let me tell you, you were right to retreat. There's more day-to-day misery about it than I could possibly describe to you." And she gave that angry little laugh again, as though ashamed of herself for having expressed such intensity of feeling.

"And so you're going to marry the likeable man with the nice taste in diamonds? I hope he realises his good fortune, Liebling. I hope he is a connoisseur of beautiful things, and knows that his future wife has the loveliest hair and probably the loveliest eyes in London."

Her laugh was less strained that time.

"I hardly think he works things out that way. He thinks I'll make a good wife and mother, and an excellent hostess in his lovely house overlooking—— Well, perhaps I won't say where it is."

"I shouldn't," he agreed. "After all, we're doing our best to remove all identity marks. And you—how do you like the rôle?"

She shrugged and smiled at him.

"I like the idea of being able to go to the opera when I like—to theatres and concerts and art shows.

Always to wear beautiful clothes, and not to feel the end of the world has come if something happens to one's only good dress. To eat well and drink well—not because I'm specially greedy, but because there's something so satisfying in perfection. To travel first class, to go to the Continent when the weather is horrid here, to toy with the delicious alternative of going by air or by luxury liner to places that are just names to me now. Oh, but you know all the things as well as I do."

"Yes, Liebling, I know." His dark eyes watched her rather sombrely. Watched the pink streak that had appeared in her cheeks, the sparkle in those dark blue eyes, the way she moved her hands, slightly but with most telling effect to emphasise what she meant.

"Why do you watch me like that?" she said as she had before. "You're thinking that a mercenary woman is even more—regrettable than a mercenary man, aren't you?"

"No, my dear, I'm thinking it's about time we fetched that letter of yours. All these Continental trips and beautiful clothes and good food rather depend on it, you know."

"Oh, yes—of course." She stood up, pushing back her chair. "You've been—awfully good to me."

"No, don't start making farewell speeches yet. It isn't—quite over," he said.

"Of course not." She gave a nervous little laugh. "We have to see if the light is still on first." He saw that her anxiety was beginning to outweigh her pleasure again, and that curiously gentle expression came back into his eyes.

"Come." He held out his hand to her. "We shall have to go back into the other room."

The hand she gave him was cold, and his fingers

curled round it comfortingly. She went to put on the light as they entered the room, but he said:

"No, no, we mustn't show any light from our window while we're doing our investigating."

"Of course not." She was a little breathless to think she could have neglected such an elementary precaution, and pushed the door to behind them with her disengaged hand, so that even the faint light from the hall should not show.

"There's no need to be frightened," he told her quietly.

"I'm *not* frightened."

"No?" He was smiling, she thought, from his tone. "Just a little, I think. But there's no reason to be. I shall fetch that letter, you know."

"You won't!"

She turned quickly and put her hands against him in the dark, almost as though she thought he would go that moment and must be stopped.

"Oh, yes, I think so."

"I won't let you. I won't let you!" Her hands pressed against him in her urgency, and at that his arms were suddenly round her. "It's *my* business. I won't have you take risks for me."

He laughed softly out of the darkness and said:

"Does your heart often beat like this?"

"My—heart? How do you know it's beating?"

"Because, darling, my hand is against it."

She felt the slight pressure of his fingers on her side, and something seemed to tighten in her throat.

"It isn't beating any harder than yours," she said in quick protest.

"Mine? I haven't got a heart," the half-laughing voice told her.

"You have. I can feel it." She moved her hand against him.

"Don't do that or I shall kiss you."

Quite deliberately she moved her hand again, and the next moment his lips were on hers in a long kiss, and then, very lightly, against her throat.

"Ah, Liebling," he gave a long sigh. "What a pity that, though we have only a few scruples, at least we cling to those."

"Why do you say that?" she said in a whisper.

"Because if we had none at all, you would stay here with me to-night."

She lay there in his arms, aware of the strength and yet gentleness with which he held her—breathless, wordless at what he had said. And then the pregnant moment of silence was shattered by a peremptory "rat-a-tat-tat" at the front door of the flat.

## CHAPTER TWO

"WHAT'S that?" Her terrified whisper seemed to pierce the darkness with a sharp edge.

"Be quiet!" His voice was low but urgent and he held her still against him.

After a few moments the knock was repeated, and this time there was also the "tr-r-ring" of the electric bell.

"I must go." He spoke curtly. "Only someone who knew me would make such a row to get in at this time of night. Get behind that curtain. We can't afford to excite the kind of curiosity there'd be if I refused to answer the door."

"But whoever it is will think you're out." She clung to him in terror.

"No. The hall porter will have said I'm in, or would do so on enquiry." He almost pushed her behind the curtain, switched on the light, and went into the tiny hall of the flat, just as a knock sounded for the third time.

Hilma flattened herself into the angle of the window, trying to remain perfectly still, and as she did so, she noticed subconsciously that a light was still shining from the window of the flat above.

She could hear nothing but a murmur of voices from the hall, but whoever the visitor was, her host was unable to get rid of him. A moment or two later she heard the voice which she now felt she knew so well say:

"Well, come in here for a moment, will you? I'll tell you anything I can, but I'm afraid I probably can't help you."

In here! He was bringing the visitor in *here*! He must be mad, Hilma thought. Then she remembered. The tell-tale table in the other room was laid for two.

"Now, Sergeant, sit down, won't you? Cigarette?"

Sergeant! This was a call from the police! Hilma's heart began to beat in slow, heavy thuds that threatened to choke her.

She gathered from the sounds that the seat was accepted, but the cigarette was not. She dared not peep between the curtains and use her eyes, but her hearing seemed all the sharper in consequence.

"Well, sir, it's a nasty business. A gentleman in this block of flats has been killed, and in pretty suspicious circumstances. Gentleman in the upstairs flat, as a matter of fact. Just above this one."

For a moment Hilma thought she was going to faint and fall forward into the room.

He was dead! Charles was dead all the time. That light which shone out into the night was blazing forth the fact. Someone else had crept up that fire-escape before her. Someone else. She shuddered and glanced through the window at the faint outlines of the iron steps outside.

But that was just being fanciful and stupid. Perhaps whoever had done it had come in boldly by the door. Perhaps it wasn't even murder.

The same idea seemed under discussion now.

"Murder, do you mean?" the cool, concerned voice of her host enquired. "Or suicide?"

"Well, sir, it wasn't suicide unless the gentleman was a contortionist. It's difficult for a man to stab himself between the shoulders."

"Oh, very, I should say. Martin was the name, wasn't it?"

"Yes, sir. The porter identified him. But I'd like to ask you a few questions. Just routine, of course."

"Of course."

"May I ask if you knew the gentleman at all, sir?"

"No, not at all. I knew him by sight, and I suppose I'd gathered a few things about him from casual observation."

"Such as?"

"Well, that he often went out late at night, entertained a good deal, and was frequently away for the week-end."

"How did you gather all that, sir?"

"Simply from the fact that you can hear footsteps pretty well from the flat overhead. When he has a party, I'm not in much doubt about it. Pretty rowdy type of party, anyway. And when there isn't a sound all the week-end, I suppose, thankfully, that he's away. But, of course, the porter can tell you all this.

I'm afraid I don't know anything exclusive about his habits."

"No, but——You say one hears things pretty well from one flat to another."

"Pretty well. Nothing in the way of odd footsteps, of course, but when there are a lot——"

"Exactly, sir. Or if someone fell heavily—you'd hear that, I dare say."

There was a reflective pause.

"Yes, I suppose you would certainly hear that. If there was no special noise going on in this flat, that is."

"Quite. You've been at home all this evening, sir?"

"Since about—eight o'clock, I should say."

"Alone?"

Again that slight pause.

"Does that matter?"

"I was only thinking, sir, that if you hadn't been talking with anyone, you'd be more likely to hear anything."

"I see. Alone—yes."

"You'll excuse me, sir, but when I passed the dining-room the door was open. I think the supper table was laid for two."

Hilma wondered if she gasped out loud. But before any reply could be made to the sergeant's facer another voice broke in on the proceedings. The front door must have been left ajar, and now what seemed to be the occupant of another of the flats burst in.

"I say, old man, this is a bad business, isn't it? Oh, there you are, Constable—Sergeant, I mean. Making your inquisition here, too. Looks as though it must be murder, you know. Well, I'm not surprised. I was just telling the sergeant here that Martin went in for a pretty gay life, all things considered. Lots of lady friends, and not above making a bit of money out of them, if you ask——"

"You'll excuse me, sir," the sergeant's voice was very curt, "but I'm busy questioning this gentleman now. I must ask you not to interrupt."

"Oh, of course. I only meant——"

But the sergeant had already turned away, an idea of some importance apparently having struck him.

"This window must lead straight on to the fire-escape, I think. If you don't mind——"

"No, just a moment." There was something very sharp in that. "Look here, there's something a little—delicate which I must explain to you." Perhaps the slight pause was supposed to give the third person a chance to withdraw. If that was so the manœuvre failed. There were no sounds of retreating footsteps.

"Yes, sir?" The sergeant's tone was encouraging but remarkably grave.

"I'm afraid I was not entirely truthful when I said I'd been alone here. As a matter of fact, I had a friend here to supper—a lady friend, you understand."

"Exactly, sir. I suppose that was her cloak lying over the chair in the other room?"

"Really"—there was a short laugh—"I congratulate you. You are remarkably observant."

"Part of our job, sir." The man's tone was stolid.

"Of course. Then I suppose it's part of your job, too, to know that one doesn't always want to advertise the presence of a supper guest—particularly at this hour."

"Bit awkward for a married man, sir."

"Or even an engaged one."

"Yes, I understand. But *you'll* understand, sir, that my business is to interrogate any strangers in this block of flats as well as the residents. I suppose the lady is behind those curtains. I'm afraid she'd better come out and let me talk to her."

There was nothing else to do, of course. Hilma put aside the curtain and came out into the room, a little pale with chagrin and nervousness, but remarkably calm.

It would have been hard to find anything more humiliating than to have to face the police sergeant, her host of the supper party and the astounded-looking third man in these circumstances. Surely, surely this need not have been forced on her?

But her common sense told her it had been the only thing to do. Two seconds later the police sergeant would have discovered her, crouching behind curtains by a window which gave on to a fire-escape leading straight on to the murdered man's flat. Her position was not a pleasant one now. It would have been ten times more suspicious without the suggestion that they were only trying to conceal a disreputable little supper-party.

"Good evening, madam. I'm sorry to have to disturb you." The sergeant was also remarkably calm about it. One would have thought he was used to finding half the witnesses in his cases hiding themselves in odd corners. But he was a man of considerable discretion, too, it seemed, for he turned to the other visitor and said, "We're rather anxious to keep everyone in their own flats at the moment, sir. Perhaps you wouldn't mind returning to yours?"

The man turned away at once and went out of the flat but, oddly enough, the glance he gave at the owner of the flat was not one of scandalised amusement, but of astonished indignation. Hilma felt it was remarkably officious of him in the circumstances.

"Now, may I have your name and address, please?" The sergeant set briskly to work.

"May I write them down?" She knew that must sound strange, but one fact had imprinted itself on her consciousness throughout the whole of her adventure. She must not—*must* not allow the repercussions of this to follow her home.

Without a word, the sergeant handed her a sheet from his notebook, and showed no surprise whatever as she wrote down the required information.

"About what time did you arrive here?"

"About half-past ten—a quarter to eleven."

"Did you see the door porter as you came in?"

There was another pregnant silence, then her companion of the evening said casually, regretfully:

"I'm afraid we'd better be quite frank with the sergeant, my dear."

"Very well." It was almost a whisper. She wondered what he expected that frankness to cover. But apparently he was prepared to make the explanations himself.

"You see"—his air of regretful embarrassment was perfect—"as I told you, this litte—escapade would be rather difficult to justify to my fiancée, and we had to take what one might call unusual precautions. The most awkward part of all was that her cousin happens to occupy the flat opposite mine. In fact, unfortunately, he is the gentleman who forced himself upon us just now."

The sergeant's almost soundless whistle was not the only comment on this statement. Hilma gave a slight gasp of sheer dismay. Only the man who was speaking seemed to be unmoved.

"In consequence, I took the rather unconventional course of asking my friend to use the fire-escape rather than the public hall and lift."

The sergeant's face became a shade more stolid.

"You don't know this lady very well, do you, sir?"

"What makes you think that?"

"The very obvious fact that you don't even know her name. She chose to write it down for me, with you as the only other person in the room."

"Oh, very well." He gave that short, annoyed laugh again. "But one doesn't always ask a girl her name before enjoying supper with her."

"Possibly not, sir." One gathered that it was, however, an invariable rule of the sergeant himself to do so. "But—you'll understand I have to ask this question—you are, I take it, *absolutely certain* that this lady approached your flat from below and not from above?"

"Beyond any question."

Hilma herself was astounded at the quiet certainty of that. How could he know, anyway? Wasn't he himself harbouring a few doubts by now? The position was queer enough, in all conscience.

Perhaps the sergeant thought such confidence peculiar too, because he said carefully:

"Why are you so positive on that point?"

"Because I watched her come up myself. We made the—the appointment earlier in the evening, you understand. I came in the usual way, having told her how to come up, and that I should be waiting at the window after the church clock there struck half-past ten. We followed that out exactly, and I saw distinctly her approach from below. Incidentally there was a light coming from Martin's window then, and, in view of what you have discovered, I suppose it still is. My friend would hardly have been likely to let herself out of a lighted window, where she would be conveniently silhouetted for anyone to see."

"Thank you, sir. You say there was a light coming from that window at ten-thirty?"

"Yes."

"Do you confirm that, madam?"

"Yes. I specially noticed it because it made—made it easier for me. Threw the rest of the staircase into deep shadow."

"Yes, I see. And you neither of you heard anything suspicious from the flat overhead during the evening?"

"No," they replied in unison, and the sergeant's expression said as plainly as possible: "Too busy, I suppose."

Hilma felt unhappily that she was being rapidly reduced to the level of an exceedingly disreputable person. "A Piccadilly pick-up" was how she put it to herself. But was it not better to be thought even that than to admit that she had actually been making her way, via the fire-escape, to the murdered man's flat?

The sergeant was consulting the notes he had made, and seemed to have come to the end of his questions.

"All right, I think that's all just now. I must ask you not to leave for another half-hour, until we've completed our examination."

"Very well." And then, as he was turning away, Hilma found the courage to enquire nervously: "Will it be necessary for—for my family to hear of this? You understand that I—it would be very awkward for me if they did."

"Yes, of course." The sergeant regarded her gravely. "I couldn't really say, madam, because it naturally depends entirely on the progress of the case. But you can rest assured that we don't stir up trouble if we can help it."

"I see. Thank you. Of course, I do understand that the whole thing must seem very queer to you. I mean—it's a rather odd sequence of events in view of what has happened."

"I daresay it isn't the only odd thing that's happened in these flats," was the sergeant's final dry comment as he took his departure. And certainly, since a murder had just taken place there, his comment seemed justified.

When he had gone there was silence for a moment or two between the two he had left behind.

Then she said very softly:

"I'm terribly, terribly sorry. I don't know what to say."

"My dear, it was hardly your fault."

"Oh, yes. I forced my way in here. However inadvertently, I *did* break into your flat and bring all this trouble on you."

"It was I who insisted on your staying to supper."

"Well, I didn't need much persuading, did I?"

"Yes, Liebling." He smiled for the first time. "I think you did, if I remember rightly. I was terribly afraid you were going to say 'No'."

She looked at him with troubled eyes for a moment. Then she too smiled faintly.

"It was just bad luck," he said with the lightest shrug. "And at least this settles the problem of fetching the letter."

"Oh!" She looked scared suddenly. "What do you suppose will happen to that?"

"I imagine the police will take over all the gentleman's correspondence, but I think a letter like that can only be signed by your Christian name?"

"Yes. But it's an unusual name."

"Any address?"

"No."

"And dated five years ago?"

She nodded. And then suddenly the most enormous relief broke over her face.

"I remember now—how silly to forget—it's just signed with a silly nickname I had then, not my real name at all."

He smiled.

"And yet you were afraid of your fiancé seeing it?"

"He knew the nickname, too. Besides, he would have known my writing."

"Liebling, don't you think you were a little foolish to give our friend the police sergeant a specimen of your writing?" She saw he had been just a little chagrined that, even in these circumstances, she had refused to disclose her identity to him.

"No. I printed the name and address."

The quickness of that amused him, of course.

"Block capitals, for the sake of clearness, eh?"

"Exactly." She smiled too.

"So that there's absolutely no way in which the police could connect that unfortunate letter with you?"

"Absolutely no way at all."

"Well then, my dear, I think you may consider yourself free from the shadow of blackmail. I only hope," he added grimly, "that we shall not be touched by a darker shadow still."

"You don't think that's—likely, do you?"

"No, not at all. It was a pity we had to use the fire-escape, that's all."

Hilma came closer to him then, and almost timidly put her hand on his arm.

"You didn't think—just for one moment—that perhaps I did have something to do with it, did you?"

He very gently raised the hand to his lips.

"No, Liebling. Such an unworthy thought never entered my head."

"It might have, you know."

"Not if I exercised a little common sense as well as blind trust." His dark eyes sparkled mischievously. "If you had been murdering someone in the way upstairs, you would hardly have paused on the way down to rob someone else's desk, you know."

She laughed. "No, I suppose not." Then her face became deadly serious again.

"But we haven't said anything of the most dreadful part of all," she cried suddenly. "Was that man *really* your fiancée's cousin?"

"I'm afraid so."

"Oh, but what will he do?"

"Well, at least he's not at all the blackmailing type."

"No, no. But he was shocked—outraged at the discovery, you know. It was written all over his face. He may think it his duty to say something."

"He may." That was very dry.

"But he *mustn't!* You must let me explain to him."

"What would you explain? That you broke into my flat by mistake because you were going to retrieve a blackmailing letter from the man who has been murdered? Oh, no, my dear, you couldn't tell that story."

"No, perhaps not exactly that, but——"

"Listen. You'll not say anything at all. As a matter of fact, he's supposed to be going to America on the V.C. 10 in the morning. If this wretched business doesn't prevent his going, then the danger of anything being said to Ev—to anyone is almost non-existent."

"You are sure?"

"Quite sure."

"But he could write," she protested, the concern still not leaving her face.

He shook his head.

"Oh, no. I know him moderately well. He's the kind of man to let anything slip out in the way of casual gossip, but not the kind to sit down and deliberately write a circumstantial account of anything."

She did look less agitated then. And when he lightly covered the hand which rested again on his arm, she gave a little gasp and the air of strain left her.

"Then you think we can really feel safe?" She passed her other hand over her forehead. "It seems too much to dare to assume after all this. One feels——"

But before he could reply, another knock at the door announced the return of the sergeant.

"Stay here. I'll go."

She stood there in the middle of the lighted room, staring round—a little stupidly, she felt, from sheer fatigue.

In front of her was the desk with the splintered lock, where she had made her first clumsy attempt at burgling. In that room beyond stood the remains of the supper she had eaten in such unconventional—even romantic—circumstances. From the hall came the sound of the police sergeant's voice speaking to her unknown host.

Except for these actual facts, she would have been tempted to think she had dreamt the incredible events of this night. But there had been no dream about it. The whole strange tangle had existed—and she still might be caught in it.

She heard the sergeant say, "Well, good-night,

sir"—and then the front door closed, and, weary though she was, she ran eagerly into the hall.

"Well?" She spoke sharply.

He smiled.

"I think this is the answer to your question about whether we could feel really safe. The sergeant says you may go home now. The doctor has been, and according to him there's no question but that Martin has been dead at least twenty-four hours. That rather lets you out of the case, doesn't it? The police aren't likely to have look you up as a witness or anything else."

"Oh!" She gave a great gasp of relief and leant against the side of the door. There was silence for a moment, then she said, almost timidly: "I can go home, then?"

"Yës, Liebling, you can go home."

She noticed at that moment that his eyes, too, looked strangely tired. Well, he also had had a sufficiently exhausting evening, she supposed.

He fetched her cloak and put it round her, fastening it for her as though she were a child.

"This is the end," thought Hilma, with the utmost sense of desolation in her heart. She could not make herself realise that it was also the end of danger, of fear, of the shadow which had threatened her for so long. She could only think of this as the end of what he had called their "short and lovely and faintly melancholy moment."

"You need not be frightened any longer," he said gently, perhaps misreading the shadow in her eyes.

"No. I know."

"May I take you down and find you a taxi?"

But she shook her head.

"No, the hall porter will do that."

"But I should like to." There was something oddly like pain in the little frown of protest.

"Much better not, you know. Let's say good-bye here—and leave it at that."

He made a slight gesture to indicate that he yielded.

She looked up at him, her hands nervously clasping and unclasping.

"You know how much I want to thank you, don't you?"

"My dear, whatever for?" He smiled down at her. "In the end, I didn't even fetch the letter."

"But you *would* have done. You were willing to do that—for me."

"Quite willing."

"I suppose," Hilma said a little breathlessly, "it would be very wrong and foolish of me to kiss you at this moment?"

"And I suppose," he retorted softly, "that we've done so many wrong and foolish things this evening that one more could hardly matter."

Very gently he took her face between his hands.

"Good-bye, Liebling," he said, and kissed her with extraordinary simplicity.

"Oh!" With a lack of poise that was foreign to her, Hilma flung her arms spontaneously round his neck. "Good-bye," she said. "Good-bye, my charming unknown."

Then she pulled herself away, jerked open the door of the flat, pulled it shut after her, and ran down the passage to the lift.

Downstairs the hall porter summoned a taxi for her by telephone, and then, as she stood there waiting for a moment or two, he remarked with melancholy relish:

"Dreadful business, this murder, madam, isn't it?"

Hilma agreed absently and then looked at him curiously.

Oddly enough, this was *his* great night, too, she realised suddenly. There he was—night porter at a block of flats where a real, first-class murder had been committed. His photograph might even appear in the Sunday newspapers. Certainly he would be questioned respectfully by many. And to as many more he would be able to remark with important casualness, "Dreadful business, this murder, isn't it?"

Happy man! For his little flame of pleasure and excitement would burn some days longer. Hers had flickered and died away, and the world was a colder place.

For a moment she was sorely tempted to say carelessly:

"What's the name of the gentleman living at 411?"

But, of course, she could not. *He* had no possible way of finding out anything about her. It was not for her to use the unfair advantage which she had.

Besides, what was the good? It was over. As completely over as a song that had been sung.

What was it he had said? That on either side lay their prosaic life. They had come from it. They must go back to it.

The taxi drew up, and with a "Good-night" to the porter she went out to it.

She gave the driver the address and got in. As she sat down the taxi started with a jerk—back to the prosaic life once more.

## CHAPTER THREE

"Hilma! Hilma!"

"Yes, Mother, what is it?"

Slowly Hilma struggled up from heavy layers of sleep. But even before she actually opened her eyes, she instinctively gave the answer that would silence that querulous repetition of her name.

"One thing is that it's very late." Her mother appeared in the doorway of her bedroom. "And the other is that that girl hasn't come."

"That girl" was Mrs. Arnall's way of referring to any one of the procession of cheap, slatternly, inefficient women who happened to be acting reluctantly as her daily help for the moment.

"Oh, dear!" Hilma sat up and pushed back her hair. "I'm sorry, Mother. How sickening for you. But perhaps she's only missed her bus."

"Oh, no." Mrs. Arnall—pretty and faded and entirely ineffectual—fretfully pulled her pink négligé more closely round her. "No, it isn't anything to do with buses. She *meant* to leave me in the lurch. I could see it, the way she tossed her head yesterday when I told her—heaven knows for the thousandth time!—about handing the vegetables at the right side."

"The left, surely?" murmured Hilma absently.

"Don't be *silly*!" Her mother sank down on the side of Hilma's bed and looked almost tearful. "You know what I mean. The right as opposed to the wrong."

"Oh, yes, I see. I wasn't thinking. I was only half awake, I'm afraid."

"Well, it's late enough, I'm sure, and there's your

father saying he must get away to the City early. Something about an important appointment—though, goodness knows, none of his appointments are important nowadays—but, anyway, he wants his breakfast, and there isn't even the kettle boiling, and I feel——"

"That's all right, Mother, I'll get breakfast. Tell Father he shall have it in a quarter of an hour." Hilma was already getting out of bed.

"Thank you, dear. I think I've got one of my heads coming on. It's all this worry about help. I'd better go back to bed. It's no good my getting really ill. We've enough expense without doctors' bills."

"Yes, you go back to bed." Hilma's voice was soothing. She knew the "heads" were as regularly recurring as the domestic crises in their family life. "I'll bring you your breakfast on a tray as soon as I've got Father off."

"Not that I really feel like *eating* anything. But one must keep going somehow." And Mrs. Arnall drifted gracefully out of the room.

Hilma was not actually dressed when she set her father's breakfast before him a quarter of an hour later, but her trim housecoat was a very different matter from her mother's trailing draperies.

"Good morning." She dropped a kiss on the top of her father's head as he sat down. "What's this I hear about an important appointment?"

"Eh? Well, well, it's too early to say much yet, of course." Her father's face lit up as Hilma sat down opposite him, leant her elbows on the table and smiled. There was something so much more heartening about a smile like that than about the really very monotonous recital of domestic woes to which he had been listening for the last half-hour. "I shouldn't be greatly surprised, though"—he buttered his toast with deliberation—"if something ve-ry, ve-ry interesting came out of this meeting."

"No? Really? How exciting! And I'm sure you will be able to handle it if anyone can."

Her father smiled. He thought so, too. No amount of failures or rebuffs of fortune had had the power to dim his certainty that "this time" everything would be well.

Hilma had seen him go off to countless "important meetings" of this sort, brushed his coat for him, watched him cock his hat at a jaunty angle. He always came back just a little dashed and puzzled for the moment. But, once he had had his tea and read the evening paper, he was able to see perfectly where things had gone wrong, and he was equally able to see why they could not fail to go right another time.

Sometimes Hilma thought it was all very pathetic. Then she used to wonder if it were possible to be pathetic if one had no realisation whatever of the disaster of things.

Mr. Arnall was a contented—even a cheerful—failure. He would never succeed at anything, but he had no idea of that. Once he had been a very rich man—through inheritance. But disastrous speculation had swept all that away some years ago. It had been a great shock at the time, but he had recovered with remarkable resilience. He realised that, inevitably, he would make his fortune again, and he had been pursuing it confidently, if unsuccessfully, ever since.

Poor Mrs. Arnall had nothing of this cheerful armour against Fate. She had been a very pretty woman, and was quite used to being petted and the centre of things. In the days of her prosperity she had been kindly and sociable and honestly wished everyone to be as happy as she was. But adversity was something she could neither understand nor cope with. She didn't really see why she should have to.

Other people were still happy and prosperous and gay. They had nice clothes, nice houses and no nightmares about quarter-day. She didn't know why her world should have changed like this, but she did know that, somehow, it was a shame.

She would have asked nothing better than to be able to be gay and sweet-tempered again, but how *could* one be with no pleasant little bridge parties, no nice theatre suppers any more, no possibility of entertaining in the really charming way she had always been used to do?

Instead, her life was made up of trying to make cheap little dressmakers understand what she meant by "line," trying to pretend that inexpensive food could be dressed up to look like the best, trying to make every kind of substitute look like the real thing, trying to make one resentful daily help do the work of three well paid good ones.

No, Mrs. Arnall had not taken kindly to reduced circumstances, and she was utterly thankful that Hilma, at least, was going to step out of all that.

It was beyond her comprehension that Tony, her adored only son, actually revelled in his horrid commercial job which had taken him away to the United States for a year's experience in the firm's office over there. She had only the vaguest idea of what work he did. She only knew that, for some unknown reason, he liked it, and contrived to manage very happily on a salary which *her* brothers would have considered insulting at his age.

"It's different for some boys, I suppose," was the only explanation she could find. But even that didn't ever seem entirely satisfactory, and she usually referred to him as "my poor Tony."

When Hilma had finally seen her father off—humming a little and even more brightly expectant than usual—she carried a breakfast tray into her mother's room.

"Here you are, Mother. Father's gone off very cheerfully."

"He always does." Mrs. Arnall sat up with a sigh and accepted her breakfast with more interest than her earlier conversation would have led one to expect.

"Shall I put on your fire for you?"

"No, dear, better not. It burns such a lot of therms or watts or whatever they are. Perhaps it's units—but anyway, they're all dreadfully expensive. And it's not *really* cold, is it?"

No, it was not, of course. That was to say, one would hardly get pneumonia sitting up in bed without a fire. Only it would have been one of those delicious, cosy little semi-luxuries which could make such a difference to the beginning of any day.

"Very well. Would you like me to bring my breakfast in here?"

"Yes, Hilma dear, do. Then we can talk over what we're going to do about help."

Hilma went away to fetch her own breakfast, and by the time she returned, she was relieved to see her mother was deeply absorbed in something other than the domestic question.

"Hilma! My dear!" She was bent over a newspaper, the sheets of which were spread haphazard over the eiderdown. "Have you seen the paper this morning?"

"No. What is it?"

"Murder!" her mother explained, dramatically if inadequately.

Hilma stiffened.

"Whose murder?"

"That's just it. I was just going to tell you. We actually knew him. Charles Martin. Do you remember? You and he were so very friendly that winter we were at Torquay. I quite hoped something would come of it. Oh, Hilma!" She looked up in horror as a new thought struck her. "What a good thing nothing *did*. You'd have been a widow now, my poor child. Though there *are* worse things," she added irrelevantly. "But a widow by murder is rather different, of course."

Hilma laughed slightly. She managed to make it quite a natural little laugh.

"You're quite right, Mother. It's a good thing my fate didn't lie in that direction."

"Oh, my dear, it is!" her mother agreed fervently, beginning to eat her breakfast, but at the same time retaining the newspaper in her disengaged hand with maddening determination.

"What do they say about it?" Hilma hoped she was not overdoing the carelessness.

"They say he was stabbed. Found stabbed in his own flat. I see they call him 'the well-known man about Town.' I don't think I should have said he was exactly *that*, would you?" Mrs. Arnall leant back against the pillows to consider this interesting point.

"Oh, I don't know. We probably shouldn't know about that, anyway. We've—lost touch with him for so long. What else do they say? Have they—do they think they've got whoever did it?"

"Well, they're a bit *mysterious* about that." Mrs. Arnall addressed herself to the newspaper once more. "They speak about 'sensational developments expected.' That probably means a woman in the case or else that they haven't the faintest idea what to think. It seems it was probably done the night before last, and the light was left on. Oh, you know, really"—her mother put down the paper again—"that does seem a frightfully careless thing for a murderer to do. It looks as though he or she—I'm sure it was she—just took panic and fled."

"Leaving the light?" There was a curious note in Hilma's voice. She could see that lighted window so well in her mind's eye.

"Yes, leaving the light. That was what first drew attention to the crime. The light being on day and night. I can't *imagine* anyone doing such a thing," declared poor Mrs. Arnall, who herself, for reasons of economy, kept the strictest watch on electric light switches.

Hilma agreed mechanically that she could not understand it either.

"Look, there's a photograph of him. I remember him *quite* well, though, of course, newspaper photographs are always hopeless. Still, you can see who it is."

With the greatest distaste, Hilma glanced at the photograph which her mother presented for her inspection. Yes, one could see who it was. She supposed that, in a cold, impersonal way, she had hated him towards the end. Those last two meetings, after a lapse of five years, had been so—so degrading. To be blackmailed was not a pleasant sensation.

But it was over now. There was no need even to think of it. Curiously, it seemed to her that she could hear a quiet, rather deep voice saying:

"Yes, Liebling, you can go home."

And that had meant that it was over.

"Well, my dear, doesn't it just *show* that one never knows." This was one of Mrs. Arnall's favourite observations on life. No one had ever been able to discover exactly what it was that "one never knew," but it usually indicated the satisfactory ending of a conversation so far as she was concerned.

In any case, the little flutter of excitement and interest had had a beneficial effect on her. She decided that, after all, she was not going to have "one of her heads," and so she would get up and face once more the latest aspect of the servant problem.

Hilma left her and went to complete her own dressing.

Curious how one tried and tried to recall a mood and a moment, and how in the brightness of daylight it became impossible.

"What was his name, I wonder?" Hilma paused in the act of brushing her hair. "Funny that it seems so important now. It isn't, of course—at all important. Roger's is the only name I have a right to consider important. Still, one can wonder. What would suit him?"

It was hard to say.

When someone came into your life in the strangest and most unconventional way, when he made the strangest—the most unconventional—impression upon you, and then went out of your life again, nameless, a little mysterious, the impersonation of that breathless feeling of romance that belonged to eighteen rather than twenty-five—well, what name could you give to him in your imagination?

She smiled faintly at her own absurdity.

But she had called him the only name possible last night. The Unknown. And even the slightly dramatic flavour about that seemed in keeping. He *was* faintly dramatic, with those great dark eyes, that quiet, commanding voice, that lightning lovemaking which might have meant anything—or nothing.

"How silly and romantic I can still be, if I'm given any chance," thought Hilma with a sigh.

But of course, real life was not a romantic business at all. It was the half-cynical, half-ruthless combination which they had discussed with such frankness last night. He had said they were sufficiently alike to understand each other's motives very well.

Well, that was quite true. She understood that he must marry his heiress, and he understood that she must marry Roger. And by common consent, they understood that it would be more than unwise for them to meet again.

"But neither of us said *why* it would be unwise," thought Hilma. And, just for a moment, she seemed to be standing again in a darkened room, with somebody's hand against her heart.

During the next few days references to "the Flat Murder" dropped to a short paragraph or two in all but the most sensational papers. One of these ventured the observation that "there seemed some support for the theory that the murdered man had engaged in more than one unsavoury activity." But nothing more explicit was ventured upon.

"Anyway, I expect that's just malicious gossip," Mrs. Arnall stated firmly. "They mean drugs, I suppose, or blackmail or something like that. But I don't feel that anyone we met at Torquay could be quite that sort."

Hilma wondered whether it was their influence or that of Torquay which was supposed to have been sufficient to preserve his virtue.

On Thursday Mrs. Arnall gave what she called "just a tiny, tiny dinner-party." Nothing at all like the smooth and sparkling affairs of happier days, of course, but just enough to please and win the approval of Hilma's grave and very correct fiancé.

In addition to Roger himself, there were only two other guests, a pretty and amusing cousin of Hilma's, named Barbara, and her husband, Jim. Barbara was considered to have done very well for herself when she had married Jim Curtis. He was "something in tin." And whatever he was in tin seemed to yield a sufficient income to maintain a remarkably smart flat in town, a small Packard, and an extensive and becoming wardrobe for his wife.

He was a good-humoured, entirely unpretentious young man whose chief idea of enjoyment was that a lot of people should "get together" and do something. It never seemed to Hilma that it mattered much what they did, so long as they all did it.

But everyone liked him, and he and Barbara were among the few people left whom Mrs. Arnall would allow herself to entertain with enjoyment untinged by worried embarrassment.

"I always remember him with gratitude when I think of that French au pair we had," she told Hilma. "Do you remember? The *soufflé* came in looking like something not very nice to drink, and he somehow made a joke, and carried the whole thing off perfectly. Dear, dear! She was a dreadful girl, and such a smasher too."

Hilma said that she thought she remembered the incident (which was not strictly correct), and then went to dress for dinner. She knew Roger specially liked the dress she chose. Dark blue, very simply and slenderly cut, the sleeves slashed from shoulder to wrist to show a lining of a much lighter blue.

She looked at herself in the glass, and again words drifted back to her from that strange evening which she sometimes thought she had imagined.

"I hope he is a connoisseur of beautiful things, Liebling, and knows that his future wife has the loveliest hair and probably the loveliest eyes in London."

Oh, dear! Was she going to remember *everything* he had said? And such an extravagant remark, too. Roger would have considered it almost indecent to have himself described as a connoisseur of beautiful things where his fiancée was concerned.

But then Roger probably never noticed that the lighter blue on her sleeves was just the blue of her eyes or anything like that. He merely thought it a nice dress and that it suited her somehow. But someone *else* would have noticed it—would have commented on it, teased her about it, told her once more that her eyes were beautiful.

"They are rather nice," Hilma said aloud. But they were very serious—almost sombre—blue eyes that regarded her from the mirror. And it was a very serious Hilma who went downstairs to receive her fiancé's conventional, but nonetheless sincere, compliments.

"Hello, Hilma, my dear." He kissed her. "You're looking very well." He referred impartially to her state of health and her looks in that remark, but Hilma, taking a modest view of it, said that—yes, she was very well.

"I meant this, too." He touched her soft pink cheek with a smile, and she was suddenly astounded to find what a difference there could be in the way a man touched one. "You've a very pretty colour to-night, Hilma. And I like that dress."

"Do you? Yes, so do I. There's something very attractive about the blue."

She waited to see if he would rise to it, but he just nodded vaguely and said, "Yes, blue's always a nice colour." And then she wanted to laugh. But above all, she wanted to have someone *with* it just as funny as she did.

Poor Roger! It was too bad. How could one expect

him to start giving voice to romantic absurdities at this date? It was not his fault, but *hers,* that everything seemed a little flat and dull just now.

Then her mother came in and, a few minutes later, her father, carrying the evening paper.

When greetings had been exchanged and they were all sipping their sherry, Mr. Arnall remarked:

"Curious business, that flat murder. They had the inquest to-day. A good deal came out then. We knew him, you know, quite well," he added to Roger, a little as though there were some distinction about it.

"Well, some years ago, my dear," his wife amended rather hastily. She seemed to feel one could be just a little indelicate in claiming too close an acquaintance with someone who had been murdered. "We met him on holiday. You know how one does."

Roger appeared to know how one did.

"It seems it was a woman who did it." Mr. Arnall glanced at his paper.

"Was it?" That came very sharply from Hilma.

"A very sordid case altogether," Roger said gravely, by which he intended to indicate quite kindly but firmly that it was not the best subject for conversation with the girl he was going to marry.

But Hilma was not noticing that.

"Who was it, Father?"

"Eh? Oh, some woman he'd been trying to blackmail. He seems to have been a pretty dirty rogue, all told. She stabbed him, and then went home and gassed herself, poor devil. But she left some sort of confession that the police found."

"Oh—poor—soul," Hilma said, with the strange sensation of having escaped some terrible danger.

"Very sordid, very sordid," repeated Roger just a trifle more loudly, as though he felt they could not possibly have heard his verdict before, or they would certainly have dismissed the case.

Fortunately, just then Barbara and her husband arrived, and there was something of a diversion. But as soon as they settled down to talk again, Barbara cried:

"Didn't you know that flat murder man once, Hilma? I was almost sure I remembered the name. We all went to a New Year's Eve dance or something one time?"

"Yes, I knew him."

"Good lord! What does it feel like to have a murderer on your visiting list?" demanded Jim.

"Don't be silly, dear," his wife said. "You've got it all wrong. He wasn't the murderer, he was the corpse. And you can't have a corpse on your visiting list. He's crossed off automatically."

They both laughed a good deal at this, though Roger raised his eyebrows as high as they would go, and Mrs. Arnall said, "Barbara! Barbara!"

"Well, it's true," Barbara declared. "It was a woman who did him in, you know, Jim. Someone he'd been blackmailing. Poor thing, I'm very sorry for her, but I never can quite see the sense of creeping about with knives just because someone's kept a few silly letters from one's youth. After all, we all *write* them, don't we? I shouldn't be surprised if Hilma had written one or two to this man herself."

"I," said Roger heavily, "should be exceedingly surprised. And I'm sure, on second thoughts, you won't want to make such a suggestion against your cousin."

"Oh, well," Barbara pouted slightly, "it's not meant as seriously as all that. I'm not really taking away your character, Hilma dear."

"Of course not." Hilma smiled mechanically.

"But I don't expect Roger was the first man you kissed. And, mark my words, Roger, *you won't be the last!*"

She laughed at Roger's expression as he tried to frame a suitable answer to this, and ran on, before he could achieve his object:

"I want you and Hilma to come to this marvellous masked charity ball at Eltrincham House. You know, Lord and Lady Ordingley have lent the place for the occasion. It's in aid of one of the hospitals, or something entirely praiseworthy. The tickets are ten guineas, but gosh, won't it be worth it!"

At that moment Mrs. Arnall announced, very much too loudly, that dinner was served, and they all moved into the other room.

But Barbara was not to be moved from her point.

"You *will* come to the ball, you two, won't you? There are quite a crowd of us going. It'll be such fun, won't it, Jim?"

"Rather. About a dozen of us, anyway. We're hoping to make it twenty," Jim explained.

"Oh, I don't think running around in fancy dress with a mask on is quite in my line," protested Roger, who, although the possessor of an excellently preserved, somewhat athletic figure, was always guarding against looking a fool, and heartily disapproved of everything which he classed under "stagey nonsense."

"It isn't fancy dress, it's only masks," cried Barbara, at the same time as Hilma exclaimed:

"Oh, Roger, I'd love to go."

"Would you, my dear?" He looked surprised, but rather indulgent as well. It was very pleasant to be able to make Hilma's eyes sparkle like that, and, in an obscure way, it pleased him to know that without his money she could not possibly go, whereas with his money he could perform the pleasing miracle for her.

"That's settled, then, isn't it?" declared Barbara.

"Well"—Roger intensely disliked being hurried—"I'm not quite certain——"

"Roger, if we could manage it, I should so like it."

Hilma didn't know quite why she was so insistent. She very seldom displayed such overwhelming enthusiasm for anything. But somehow, the idea of this attracted her. Perhaps it was that the idea of a masked ball appealed to the vein of romanticism which had so recently been touched in her. Or perhaps it was just that the novelty was as charming to her as to Barbara.

In any case, it was entirely beyond Roger to resist the appeal of her flushed cheeks and shining eyes. And he said immediately—indeed, with a good deal of graciousness:

"Then of course we'll go."

"That's splendid!" Both the Curtises seemed enchanted at having increased their party still further.

"But you'll have to have a new dress, of course," Barbara added. "It's a sort of point of honour not to have oneself identified if possible. And as it's only masks and not fancy dresses, too, one must have something none of one's friends will recognise."

"Hark at her," Jim begged of the assembled company. "If there's another woman this side of heaven who can find more excuses than my wife for buying new dresses, I'd like to meet her poor devil of a husband and swop experiences." And he smiled with a good deal of pride at Barbara.

"It's not an excuse. It's perfectly true," Barbara replied imperturbably. "A new dress is an absolute necessity."

"You called it a point of honour a few minutes ago," her husband pointed out. "I'd stick to that if I were you. It's more unusual."

Hilma saw her mother biting her lip nervously at this point, and she interposed calmly with:

"All right, I'll have a new dress for the occasion. You remember the silk Aunt Gertrude gave me, Mother. That will do splendidly."

"Oh, yes, dear. Yes, of course." Her mother gave a little gasp of relief and flickered her lashes nervously.

"Poor Mother," thought Hilma. "Poor, poor Mother! She thought the whole plan was going to be ruined for the price of a new evening dress. And that we'd be humiliated, too, by having to own to the reason. Oh, I know why I'm marrying for money! How could I do anything else?"

After that, the evening went very pleasantly. The guests obviously enjoyed themselves, and the arrangements for attending the masked ball were settled beyond dispute.

When the guests had gone and Mrs. Arnall had ceased to enumerate the points on which there might perhaps have been improvement, Hilma said:

"What a good thing Aunt Gertrude sent me that length of silk, wasn't it?"

"Yes, dear. It was a horrid moment until you remembered that," her mother remarked quite simply.

Hilma smiled comfortingly.

"Well, I couldn't have anything nicer. It's a heavenly blue, you remember, with just a powdering of tiny gold flowers."

Mrs. Arnall looked very pleased. And as the dress began to take shape during the next few days, she looked even more pleased. *She* knew that Hilma was one of the loveliest girls in London (who should know it better than her own mother?) and she liked to see her daughter look her best.

With the help of a fairly humble but (as Mrs. Arnall phrased it) "quite intelligent" dressmaker, Hilma evolved a dress of considerable simplicity but of very beautiful line.

"It *is* line that counts, Hilma. Believe me, it was always the *line* that made my dresses into models in the old days when I could afford such things."

So line was duly studied in this case, too, and, as a result, the beautiful dress fitted Hilma like the proverbial flower-sheath, winning her mother's entire approval. Even her father said:

"Very pretty indeed, my dear. It's new, isn't it?"

Hilma stood smilingly before him. She was only waiting now for Roger to come and fetch her.

Hilma put on her little gold mask, and immediately it seemed to impart a faintly elusive—even mysterious—air to her whole personality. It was not only that she had done her hair differently, reflected Mr. Arnall, with a slightly troubled sigh. There were times when he felt he hardly knew his daughter quite so well as he had supposed. This was one of them.

The impression disturbed him a little. He was a man who liked his children to "remain young," as he put it to himself. He would have preferred to be able to think of her still much as he had when she was young enough to be taken to Kensington Gardens and shown the Albert Memorial.

But the golden mask didn't go with anything like that.

It was not that she was anything like so bright and glittering and modern as her cousin Barbara, for instance. Indeed, thought Mr. Arnall, who had a nice discrimination in shades of meaning, there was no glitter about her at all, because that implied something cold. There was a glow—that was the word. A warm, golden glow. But that enhanced the faintly mysterious air which she had this evening. And Mr. Arnall was not at all sure that he wanted any daughter of his to be mysterious.

Ah, well, it was a good thing she was marrying a nice, steady, unimaginative fellow like Roger Dolan. Nothing mysterious about him. And nothing mysterious about his solid income and his big house near Putney Heath, either. That was even more to the point perhaps.

Roger arrived a few minutes later.

He was still not entirely happy about the business of masks, although he admitted at once that Hilma's was beautiful and that her whole appearance was enchanting.

"But it's all very well for women, dressing up and playing the fool a little," he said. "I've *brought* a mask, of course, but I must say it all seems very ridiculous to me. I don't like making an exhibition of myself."

Hilma wondered just a little impatiently how he supposed he was going to make an exhibition of himself when he would be one of hundreds doing exactly the same thing. But she supposed it was hardly poor Roger's fault that he was singularly lacking in the carnival spirit, and it was all the kinder of him to have yielded to her wish to go.

"You're looking your very best, Roger," she told him. "Awfully nice and big and masculine. A mask won't make much difference, and everyone will be wearing one, you know. It would be terribly conspicuous not to—besides being against the rules of the evening."

Roger's horror of being conspicuous immediately

helped him to swallow that bait. If it would appear peculiar to be without a mask, then, of course, to go masked was the only thing to do.

They donned their masks—since they were supposed to arrive disguised—and went out to Roger's car, Roger muttering that he hoped his chauffeur would not think they had taken leave of their senses.

The chauffeur naturally had no such idea. He had once been chauffeur to an aged actress who had spent the last ten years of her life trying to recapture her youth. It would have taken a great deal more than a couple of masks to arouse even the mildest curiosity in him.

"Oh, Roger, it's going to be such fun!" Hilma turned to him in the car and smiled at him. And even Roger thought how strange and beautiful her blue eyes looked as they sparkled at him through the gold of her mask.

"I'm glad you think so, my dear," was what he said. But he honestly meant it. He *was* glad if she was pleased—only Hilma wished there were someone to share her gay, rather crazy mood of the moment. There was nothing either gay or crazy about Roger.

The house where the ball was being held was magnificent, with grounds that once would never have imagined a London house could boast. The whole setting was gorgeously suitable to the occasion, and even Roger began to blossom forth slightly when he found that literally everyone else there seemed very willing to "dress up and play the fool a little," as he had said.

The windows of the great ballroom came right to the floor, and they had been opened outwards on the warm dusk of an early autumn evening. The lilt of music, the ripple of talking, the bubble of laughter made an irresistible combination, and there *was* something slightly intoxicating about the adventurous feeling it gave one to know that identity was put in doubt—if not entirely destroyed—by the absurd and delightful masks. Perhaps Roger didn't quite catch the full enjoyment of it, but at least he began to think it a nice evening.

To Hilma the enjoyment was almost painfully intense. She realised obscurely that during the last week or so she had had a great longing to escape from reality—to run away from the hard, rather heavy actualities of life. This evening she seemed to have achieved something like that escape. Nothing was completely real. Not even Roger. For how could Roger be completely real in a mask?

From time to time during the evening she danced with other men. Men whom Barbara—who had insisted on disclosing her quite undisguisable identity—brought up and introduced in a cheerful, casual way which left one quite unaware of their real names. But to Hilma it seemed that the highlight of the evening had been reached when—Roger having left her to fetch her an ice—she stood by one of the long open windows, savouring the quiet of the night outside yet keenly aware of the gay scene in the room.

The contrast accorded very well with her mood—half-gay, half-melancholy. She stood with her back against the shutter of the window, her eyes on the little slice of golden moon that was creeping up the sky. She was half lost in a reverie of her own when a voice spoke softly beside her.

"Liebling," the voice said, and she started at the sound of it, for that caressing tone with the undercurrent of laughter could belong to only one person. "Liebling, is it possible that I've found you again?"

## CHAPTER FOUR

FOR a moment Hilma was so startled and so thrilled that she could not have turned round, anyway. Then a strangely mischievous little impulse took hold of her.

"Don't you think," she said softly in return, "that you've made a mistake?"

"No, Liebling. I have watched you for too much of this evening. Do you think I don't know that wonderful hair—even though you have it piled up in that delicious, ridiculous way on top of your head? Besides, a mask doesn't hide the eyes, you know."

She didn't answer that directly. She said instead:

"My fiancé will be coming back in a moment."

"Yes, I'm sure of that. Come with me into the grounds."

"I—can't very well. Besides, I don't know the way."

"I do. And you know we must talk. Please, Liebling—while there's still time."

"All right. You go, I'll follow you. Which is the way?"

"Throught the door on the left at the end of the room, and then down the little flight of steps."

She hardly let her glance follow him, but she knew he had gone from her side. Then she was seized with panic lest she should not get away herself before Roger came back. He would wander about looking for her, of course. Get very worried and a good deal annoyed.

Oh, well, let him! she thought, with sudden reckless impatience. And she began to thread her way through the people at the side of the room.

Near the door she ran into Barbara and, catching her by the arm, said coolly:

"If you see Roger, tell him I've torn my dress a bit and gone to the cloakroom to have it put right."

"Very well. Is it serious? Pity—such a pretty dress."

"No, nothing much, but it may take a little while. He would wonder where I was."

"All right, I'll tell him," Barbara said, and Hilma passed quickly out of the door on the left.

A short flight of steps lay straight in front of her, and at the bottom she could see a glass door which evidently led out of doors.

Running down the steps, she pushed open the door and stepped out into the darkness. At the sudden change from the light she could see only vague shapes round her. Then someone caught her hand and a voice said:

"Come this way, down the yew alley. There's a stone bench at the end."

She caught her breath on a little laugh of sheer excitement, and at that he laughed too.

"How do you know the place so well?" she said in a whisper, because somehow the dark shapes of the yew trees were mysterious and a trifle frightening.

"I used to stay here sometimes as a boy. I'm remotely related to the owner of the place."

"Oh, I see."

"Look, here's the bench. Now, sit there, where I can see you in what little moonlight there is. You're not cold, are you?" He touched her bare arm very lightly and gently.

"No," she said, and hoped he didn't notice her slight shiver of excitement.

"Aren't you going to take off your mask?" She saw how his eyes were sparkling through the eye-holes of his own mask.

"No," Hilma told him, "I don't think I am. That's outside the rules of the evening."

"Oh, I'm sorry for that." He leant back with his arms folded, and she saw his mouth, below the line of his black mask, curve with something like indulgent amusement.

"Why? Don't you like it?" She was faintly chagrined.

"It's beautiful, Liebling. But it makes you a little frightening."

"Frightening?" She was taken aback. "But why should it?"

"It gives you a remote and unearthly character. Like one of those beautiful princesses of Egypt who have death-masks of pure gold."

"Oh!" She snatched the mask from her face. "I think that's a horrible thing to say."

He laughed.

"But it had the desired result," he told her, and at that, her reluctant smile came. "Besides, Liebling, I think it serves you right for that horrid moment when you pretended not to know me," he added gravely.

Hilma laughed then.

"Did you really think then that you'd made a mistake?" she enquired irresistibly.

But he shook his head.

"You said—you said you'd watched me for a long time."

"Yes. You and the big fair man with the slightly self-conscious air. I suppose that's the fiancé?"

"Yes. He doesn't really like wearing a mask, poor Roger. He thinks it's very silly."

"So it is—a little. That's why you and I like it."

She laughed.

"Perhaps that's true."

"So that's—Roger?" he said reflectively. "He looks, I'm sorry to say, an entirely worthy person. A thoroughly good sort."

"He *is*. Why shouldn't he be?"

"Oh, no reason at all. Except that he's a very large and very solid reproach to anyone as frivolous and unstable as I am."

"Yes," Hilma agreed. "Yes, I suppose that's how he makes me feel sometimes. That's the worst of being a second-rate person, isn't it?"

"Eh? Yes. Yes, of course it is."

There was a slight pause while they digested that. Then she said:

"I suppose we *are* definitely inferior people to Roger?"

"Unquestionably. I'm afraid." And she saw again the roguish sparkle of his eyes behind the dark mask.

"Tell me, is—is *she* here to-night too?"

"Evelyn?"

"Oh—her name's Evelyn, is it?"

He nodded.

"Yes, she's here."

"Could I—pick her out from description? Or is that against the rules?"

"No, it isn't against the rules. Since I've met Roger—metaphorically speaking, of course—I see no reason why you shouldn't meet Evelyn—also metaphorically speaking. She's slim and dark and is wearing a red dress. Altogether I should call her the smartest-looking girl in the room, I think," he added thoughtfully.

"Oh, would you?" Hilma was surprised to find how little she liked that. "How—nice for you to have such a smart fiancée."

"Except, Liebling," he said with an odd touch of weariness, "that smartness is not a quality which appeals to me above all others."

She wondered curiously which quality did, but forbore to ask him.

"Anyway"—she spoke a little coldly—"beggars can hardly be choosers."

"Perfectly right, Liebling." He seemed genuinely amused by the feel of her claws. "Perfectly right, but most unpleasantly expressed."

"I'm sorry!" She felt much more contrite than she could have wished. "I was—I was thinking of both of us, you understand."

"I'm honoured to be coupled with you in anyone's thoughts," he assured her. But, feeling suddenly at a disadvantage, she said quickly:

"Aren't you going to take off your mask, too?"

He took it off at once. But she thought that his eyes were not so sparkling without the setting of the mask. They looked tired, somehow, and just a little disillusioned.

"Well, we haven't either of us many illusions, I suppose," thought Hilma. And at that moment he spoke again.

"The case of our blackmailing friend seems to have settled itself satisfactorily. There can hardly be any reason for the police to take any further interest in either of us."

"No," Hilma agreed. And then, with a sigh: "Wasn't it terrible?"

"What? The whole experience, do you mean?"

"Oh, *no*!" She found she didn't mean that at all. "No, I was thinking of that poor woman, feeling so desperate—ten times more desperate than I felt, I suppose. And she *didn't* mistake the flat, or find the problem solved for her. She had to go right through with it. Right through to the point of murdering him."

"Why, Liebling," he said curiously and gently, "you never got near murder, did you?"

"Oh, no. But then I hadn't so much at stake as she, I dare say. Even if everything had gone wrong, I should have lost Roger and a very good marriage. But—suppose I had loved him desperately——" She stopped and looked away thoughtfully into the shadows.

"Are you suggesting"—his tone was mocking, but only slightly so—"are you actually suggesting that the case would then have been much more serious?"

"Oh, well——" She gave a shamefaced little laugh, as though she had only just realised she was cornered.

"Because, if so," he pointed out gravely, "you're deliberately going against the worldly and mercenary principles which you upheld to me."

"You supported them, too," she reminded him quickly.

"Of course. That's why I immediately recognised the *volte-face*," he assured her.

"It wasn't a *volte-face*," she said with a slight sigh. "I wasn't quite thinking what I was saying."

He smiled rather at this explanation.

"You know, Liebling," he shook his head regretfully, "the trouble with you and me is that we're not *complete* worldlings or egoists or opportunists, or whatever we like to call it. We have a sad streak of romanticism in us, which is continually betraying us."

"It won't have a chance of betraying me often, when I'm married to Roger," Hilma said, half to herself.

"No." He considered that gravely. "No, I don't somehow imagine Evelyn encouraging a romantic streak either." And then, with a complete change of mood: "You know, I hope she and Roger have found each other. I feel they'd have a lot in common."

Hilma laughed outright then.

"You're really very absurd," she told him. But he shrugged very slightly and smiled.

"What else should one be, Liebling, in what is, after all, a rather absurd world?"

She didn't reply to that. After a short silence she said:

"Oh, I meant to ask you. Did the cousin—Evelyn's cousin, you know—go to America after all?"

"Yes. He cleared off safely without making any compromising statements."

"He didn't—he didn't even reproach you or anything?" She still looked slightly anxious.

"Oh, no. As a matter of fact, I didn't see him again. I only heard from my manservant that he had left, according to his arrangements."

"And you're *sure* he didn't say anything—by phone, for instance—before he left?"

"My dear," he smiled rather dryly, "I can't imagine that I should have heard nothing about it from Evelyn if that was so."

"Oh, no, of course. I forgot." She gave a slight sigh. "Then it's all right?"

"It is all right," he agreed with that faintly indulgent smile for her nervousness.

"He's not coming back very soon, or anything like that?"

He shrugged.

"I'm afraid we were not intimate enough for me to have any real information about his movements."

"Then"—her eyes widened again—"then he still might turn up and make himself dangerous?"

"Liebling, is it your custom to cross *all* your fences before you come to them?" he asked with a smile.

"No." She pushed back her hair with that characteristic little gesture that always drew his gaze to her. "I was only thinking——"

"What, my dear? What were you thinking?"

"That if he did come back, and if he did think it his business to interfere, you ought to know where to find me, oughtn't you?"

"Should I, Liebling?" His smile was almost tender that time. "How sweet of you even to think of a reason why I ought to know how to get in touch with you. I feel on a level with the London police force now."

"The London police force?" She gave him a puzzled frown.

"Oh, yes. You surely haven't forgotten that you administered a very sharp snub to me. You actually wrote down your name and address for a miserable police sergeant who didn't mean anything to you, while I had to stand by and look pleasant."

"Oh, that!" she laughed. Then her eyes sparkled in their turn. "But that," she pointed out demurely, "was because I was forced to."

"Hm. Yes, I see the subtle difference. I haven't perhaps been quite autocratic enough with you."

She smiled, but the serious mood was returning now.

"No, please let's be serious for a moment. I meant what I said just now. You—you ought to know where to find me."

"And I meant to ask you—why? The delightfulness

of the arrangement I quite understand, but the necessity—no."

"Well, I told you—suppose this cousin returned and wanted to make trouble, then *I* should have to explain to him, because——"

"I told you I wouldn't have that," he said in a curt tone she had not heard from him since he discovered her rifling his desk.

"But why not? There's no danger in my being frank with him now. I couldn't be involved in the murder case—it's all explained and done with."

He looked at her in a sombre way that brought those tiny crinkles round his eyes again, and made her wonder for the first time just how old he was.

"You would have to explain to him that there was a compromising letter—blackmail—an attempt to burgle his flat. It wouldn't be very nice for you to have to tell a strange man all that," he said quietly.

"But I've already had to tell a strange man all that." The uncontrollable dimple appeared in the centre of her cheek suddenly. "A pretty horrible man, too, who threatened to send for the police if I didn't tell him the whole story."

"Oh, Liebling!" He laughed and took her hand. "Was I very brutal with you?"

She nodded, her smiling blue eyes on his face.

"Yes." He looked reflective. "I remember. I thought: 'Now don't be fooled. She's so lovely that she probably thinks she can get away with anything. Be firm with her from the beginning.' "

"How sweet! And terribly ingenuous. It goes with the 'little boy' part of you," she told him gravely.

"My God! The *what*?"

"You heard me."

"There isn't the very slightest element of the little boy about me."

She nodded emphatically, so that the moonlight glimmered palely on her bright hair.

"Yes, there is. When you wanted me to ask questions about you and show curiosity, you were just like a little boy hoping for notice. That," she added with a smile, "was why I had to do what you wanted."

"Oh, Liebling, don't." He put his forehead against the hand he was holding.

"Why not?"

"Nothing. Except that it hurts a little."

"Oh—I'm sorry." Just for a moment her other hand hovered over his bent, dark head. But she took it away again resolutely and said: "Well—well, we're getting rather far away from the name and address, aren't we?"

"I suppose we are." He looked up immediately. Then: "So you want to give me your name and address?"

"No," she said slowly, "as a matter of fact, I don't *want* to. I think it might be—might be——"

"Unwise?"

"Well—not in our best interests, shall we say? But on the other hand, I can't risk your being involved in something that might wreck your marvellous engagement, just because I wasn't there to make explanations."

"I see."

He took out a notebook, tore a leaf from it, and gravely handed her the page and a pencil.

"Suppose you write it down—as you did for our friend the police sergeant."

She took the pencil, glanced at him doubtfully for a moment, and then—seeing that he was looking away from her into the black and silver of the moonlit garden—she slowly wrote down "Hilma Arnall" and then added the address.

"Block capitals for clearness," he reminded her, smiling, but still without looking at what she was doing.

"I have," she told him. And when she looked up and saw his smiling profile, she caught herself wondering if Evelyn thought it wonderful to kiss him.

"Now fold up the paper."

Amused and faintly puzzled, she did so.

"It's done," she told him. "Is this a game?"

"No, Liebling." He turned to her then. "It's deadly serious."

He took out his pocket-book and held it open for her.

"Now put it in there—under the flap." She did so rather gravely, as though it were a matter of great moment. "I promise you," he said, with that serious smile, as he replaced the pocket-book, "that I shall not unfold that and look at it unless what you're so afraid of actually happens."

Hilma's eyes widened with sheer astonishment.

"Do you mean to say you can *keep yourself from looking at it?*"

He nodded, still with that smile.

"Well," Hilma said slowly, "I call that a pretty stiff test of character."

"I thought," he agreed gravely, "that it wasn't a bad test myself. For a second-rate person, of course."

She laughed then—softly and with much more feeling than she knew. Then with a quick sigh, she rose to her feet.

"Do you know we must go in? We've been here much too long already. I'm sure Roger must have grown tired of looking for me."

Just for a moment he sat looking up at her, as though she were a picture that one must impress on one's mind. Then he stooped and picked up a bright scrap from the path.

"Your mask, Liebling." And he held it out to her.

"Oh, of course." She was a little scared to find she had so far forgotten realities as to have been on the point of returning without her mask.

She put it on, and he stood up then, putting on his own as he did so. She was queerly, emptily conscious that he had not kissed her this time.

There was no reason why he should, of course. There was, on the contrary, every reason why he should not. But the disappointment remained, all the same.

Perhaps there was faint comfort in the fact that he held her hand as they passed through the shadows of the yew alley. But then almost immediately they reached the doorway to the stairs and he said quietly:

"Go on ahead. We mustn't go in together. Good-night, Liebling." He opened the door for her and very gently pushed her inside.

Then the door closed behind her, and she was alone on the stairs.

For a moment she had a wild, inexplicable desire to run out again into the night, away from nice, kind, dependable Roger and all he represented to—what?

Then the moment of madness passed, and she began to climb the stairs—slowly, as though she were very tired.

It was not, of course, very easy to explain so long an absence to Roger, but Barbara, who happened to be standing near him, rushed all unknowing into the breach.

"Oh, my dear, you *must* have damaged your dress badly!"

"My dress?" For a second Hilma could not even think what her dress had to do with it. But fortunately the mask hid some of the puzzlement in her eyes, and she recovered almost at once. "Yes, it was rather a business, but the attendant made a marvellous job of it. I'm so sorry, Roger, that I was missing such a long time."

Roger accepted the explanation with a moderately good grace, while Barbara secretly thought:

"Poor Hilma! She looked quite dazed. I suppose a spoilt frock is an absolute disaster to her. She wouldn't get another for ages—not till Roger starts buying them for her, most probably. It must be dreadfully humiliating. Thank goodness she's marrying money. They'll all need it."

After that Hilma danced once more with Roger. There was nothing else to do. There hadn't been at the beginning of the dance, of course, and yet there had seemed to her a sparkle and a promise of excitement in every note of the music then.

Now everything was changed. Flat, dull and pointless. Where was the sense of moving round and round to the same kind of tunes? And how silly everyone looked with a bit of material plastered across their faces. Roger had been quite right—it was a stupid business. It made one wonder even why one had come.

Then she caught sight of a slim dark girl in a wonderful wine-red frock, and her partner was tall and dark and familiar.

Hilma knew then why she had come to this dance, She had not known beforehand. How could she? But she had *had* to come, of course. Otherwise there would have been no meeting in the garden.

On impulse she said to Roger:

"Look, do you see that girl there in the red dress? Don't you think she looks wonderfully *chic* and smart?"

Roger glanced across the room.

"Oh—yes. But she has some reason to. That's Evelyn Moorhouse, you know."

"Do you mean the banker's daughter?"

"Yes. I should imagine Owen Moorhouse left her enough to buy all the smart clothes she wanted," Roger added with a laugh. "As a matter of fact, I was introduced to her while you were away just now. She's a very charming girl"

"Is she?" Hilma said, and very much wanted to laugh in her turn. So their little joke had not been quite so absurd, after all.

Then she felt her amusement fade. Evelyn Moorhouse, indeed? Well, she would be an irresistible "catch" for any genuine opportunist, of course.

Hilma was glad suddenly that it was time to go home.

When they got outside, there was the usual confusion over taxis and cars, and Hilma stood waiting for several minutes while Roger went to discover his car. She moved to the side of the great doorway, to avoid the jostle of people around her, but even as she did so a hand closed lightly round her wrist.

"Liebling"—his voice was very low indeed—"shall I see you again?"

"Oh, but I thought we'd said good-bye!" She spoke almost in a whisper, too, but her agitation was patent in her voice.

"I thought so, too. Forgive me, but——Not even once more, my dear?"

She saw suddenly some yards away a worried, rather fussing Roger making his way towards her. He had not yet picked her out in her new position, but he would at any moment. Not taking her eyes from him, she spoke in a rapid whisper.

"On Sunday afternoon. Richmond Park, near the Robin Hood Gate. Half-past three."

Still she didn't look at him. She heard him say softly, "Ishall be there." Then she moved forward through the throng to Roger.

"Oh, there you are." Roger smiled and took her by the arm. "I'm sorry I was such a long time. Half the cars in London seem to be collected round here, but I've found mine now. It's just down this side street. If you don't mind walking a little way it will be quicker than waiting until it has time to draw up."

Hilma didn't mind walking, it seemed. She didn't really mind anything. She was thinking of Richmond Park on a Sunday afternoon—near the Robin Hood Gate.

On the way home she was rather silent. But Roger didn't apparently notice anything amiss. For one thing, he was a good deal more talkative than usual himself. He had enjoyed his evening considerably more than he had expected, and now he felt very well disposed towards the world.

"It was odd, running into Toby Elton like that, wasn't it? I'd no idea he ever went to that sort of thing."

"Who was that, Roger?" She realised that her thoughts had been wandering unpardonably again. In fact, Roger looked very slightly offended.

"Toby Elton. The man I told you about. It was he who introduced me to Miss Moorhouse, you know."

"Oh, was it?" She made a valiant effort to follow intelligently. "Let me see, weren't you at Cambridge with him?"

"Yes, that was the fellow. Magnificent cricketer.

But of course, that was twenty years ago." Roger smiled reminiscently.

Twenty years ago! and a contemporary of Roger's. That did really rather make one think. Yes, she supposed, Roger must be all of forty. More than fifteen years older than she. But then one could hardly expect to have everything.

She was glad when they arrived home.

Roger kissed her good-night just before the car drew to a standstill. He never indulged in affectionate farewells unless he had first made sure that his chauffeur's attention was otherwise engaged. The chauffeur, of course, remained entirely unaware of this thoughtfulness, but at least it saved Roger a good deal of embarrassment.

Hilma silently let herself into the darkened house. She knew her mother and father would have been in bed a long while ago, but she was not specially surprised when, half-way through undressing, she heard their door creak softly.

If Hilma had been out somewhere really exciting, Mrs. Arnall usually found it irresistible to come and enquire about her evening, and, at the discreet little tap, Hilma smiled and said softly: "Come in, Mother."

Mrs. Arnall came in, in the inevitable pink wrap.

"Well, Hilma dear, how did you enjoy yourself?"

"Wonderfully." Hilma looked at her with brilliant eyes that confirmed that beyond question.

"Oh, I'm *so* glad. I do like you to go to a few decent places sometimes," Mrs. Arnall said plaintively. By "decent" places, she meant places to which they would have gone in their happier, prosperous days.

"You haven't been lying awake, waiting to hear my report, have you?" Hilma carefully drew off her best pair of tights.

"No, no, I'd been to sleep. The sound of the car woke me."

"Oh, I'm sorry, Mother."

"No, that's all right. I like to hear all about it straight away."

Hilma smiled and bit her lip. This was almost as pathetic as her father's jaunty assurance when he went off to face another failure. Her mother spoke like someone receiving news of home when in a foreign land.

"It was a gorgeous scene." Carefully Hilma tried to reconstruct it for her, describing the rooms, the dresses, even referring once to the moonlit grounds. "And there was an atmosphere of—of adventure, Mother. Rather as though anything might happen."

"I know." Her mother nodded. "So cheap and nasty when everything isn't done just so, but the nicest thing possible when it's done with taste and money."

"Yes, I suppose so." Hilma was hardly listening. She was living again some of the best moments of that evening—and they had nothing much to do with the brilliance of the scene in the ballroom.

"You know, Hilma dear"—her mother sat in a low chair, her hands thoughtfully clasped round her knee—"it gives me such a *comfortable* feeling to know that Roger can take you anywhere like that when you want to go. I should so hate to think that, after you were married, you should ever have to skimp and contrive and worry as I have done."

"Oh, Mother"—Hilma turned quickly and glanced at her compassionately—"I know. You've had a rotten time really, haven't you?"

"Well, at any rate I had a good time first," her mother admitted. "I'm never sure whether that makes it *better* or *worse*. I mean, perhaps it helps, never to have known how gay and rich and comfortable things *can* be. Or perhaps it's some sort of comfort to look back on good times and hope, however stupidly, that they'll come again. Anyway, I suppose none of these things matter so much when you're getting older, except for the day-to-day irritation of it. But when you're young——" She stopped and shook her head.

"But—don't you think—at least one has good spirits and resilience then?" There was a strange, almost pleading note in Hilma's voice when she said that. Almost as though she begged her mother to confirm some struggling little theory that was trying to find place in her own mind.

But Mrs. Arnall shook her head again—much more emphatically this time.

"No, I can't imagine anything more dreadful, Hilma, than to be young and gay, with a great capacity for enjoying oneself—and nothing whatever to enjoy. That's why I'm so thankful you're marrying a rich man. Someone who can give you your right setting. You'll be able to have lovely clothes while you're still young enough and pretty enough to set them off. You'll be able to travel at a time when enjoyment means more than comfort, and so you will feel the novelty and adventure of it all, instead of sitting about on decks or on hotel verandas watching others do the interesting things, as one does when one is older. You'll be able to plan out the best kind of education for your children without counting up how much it costs. And—and—oh, everything," finished Mrs. Arnall, vaguely but comprehensively.

Hilma looked sombrely at her mother. She knew the force of all those arguments. In speaking, her mother might put clothes first and the children's education last, but she didn't mean it too literally that way. She was arguing the case for the desirability of money—for its solid advantages as well as its frivolous pleasures.

Well, of course, there was nothing in all this that she had not told herself long ago. If one loved the good things of life—and Hilma admitted grimly that she did—it was pretty bitter to have to do without them consistently. As her mother said, perhaps it was easier never to have known them. Once one *had* know them—well, one recognised the wisdom of making sure of them for the future.

". . . So, you see, dear"—her mother had been developing her theme at some length, unknowing that Hilma was not following her—"*that* was why I was so delighted when I realised you were making up your mind to accept Roger. That and the fact that he's so extremely nice, of course," she added hastily.

"Yes, he's—an awfully good sort, you know, Mother." Then she realised suddenly that she was quoting someone else, and that that was not quite the kind of thing one said of one's fiancé, in any case. "He is a dear," she added conscientiously, and her mother earnestly agreed.

"Well, I suppose we ought to go to bed now." Hilma smiled at her mother. "It must be very late."

"Yes, of course we must. Did you meet anyone interesting there?"

Hilma had half turned away to the bed already, so that her mother could not have seen how her eyes widened and a faintly rigid look came round her mouth.

"There were one or two new friends of Barbara's—no one very special. Oh, Roger met Evelyn Moorhouse, the daughter of the banker. I wasn't there when he was introduced. He said she seemed very charming."

"Evelyn Moorhouse? Dear, dear, she must be

worth a good deal. Old Owen Moorhouse left enough, goodness knows, and I think she was the only daughter."

"Maybe." For the life of her, Hilma could not infuse any warmth into her tone. And, seeing at last that Hilma was determined to go to bed, Mrs. Arnall said good-night and left her.

Hilma got into bed, switched off the light, and lay there looking into the darkness.

"You know, Liebling," he had said, "the trouble with you and me is that we are not *complete* worldlings... We have a sad streak of romanticism in us, which is continually betraying us."

She sighed and turned over restlessly.

But then they had both agreed that, once they were married, they would have little opportunity to develop that romanticism.

Perhaps it was all right, after all.

## CHAPTER FIVE

In the middle of the next afternoon Barbara appeared, very pretty and smart in a plum-coloured trouser suit.

"Hello! I've come to talk over the evening." This was one of Barbara's specialities. She loved to hold cheerful inquests on anything she had particularly enjoyed. "Wasn't it fun, Hilma? Aunt Cecily, you can't *imagine* how marvellous it was. Aren't you glad I made you make Roger bring you?"

She turned from one to the other, asking questions

and making comments, but very seldom waiting for the replies.

"I thought Hilma looked lovely, Aunt Cecily. So sort of remote and exquisite. You did, Hilma. It was such a lovely dress. I hope there wasn't any permanent damage done, was there?"

"Why, was your dress hurt, Hilma?" Mrs. Arnall looked distressed. Hilma had never looked nicer in anything and it would be impossible to replace.

"No, Mother, nothing to speak of."

"There, I suppose I've put my foot in it," Barbara remarked with cheerful contrition. "She probably didn't mean to tell you anything about it, Aunt Cecily. I forgot. Of course, one doesn't tell mothers that sort of thing. However sweet they are—and you *are* sweet, Aunt Cecily—they feel it's their duty to be shocked. I shouldn't have told Mother, now I come to think of it. But when you're married it's different. You'll find it is, Hilma. If you harm your things then—well, you've only got yourself to moan to. And anyway, you'll be all right with Roger. He's the kind who'll quite enjoy buying you new things. Start training him as you mean to go on. I did with Jim. And now he's just as interested as I am in what his wife looks like." And Barbara laughed contentedly.

"Are you *sure* it wasn't much hurt, Hilma?" enquired poor Mrs. Arnall, who could not bring herself to dismiss it all so gaily as this. "Was it torn? Or was something upset on it?"

"It was torn. Only a little—nothing that mattered."

"Where was it torn?"

"Oh—just at the—at the waistline where the gathers come. The attendant in the cloakroom stitched it back perfectly. There's nothing to worry about," Hilma explained hastily. She found she very much disliked inventing like this to her mother.

"Well, if you're sure?"

"Yes, quite sure."

"There were some awfully interesting people there," struck in Barbara again, apparently under the impression that Hilma's damaged dress had already occupied its fair share of the conversation. "The new Earl and Countess of Carbrough, and Julie Fox. Marvellous! She's gone blonde again. And Edward Maine. They say the camera can't lie, but I must say he looks ten years older off the screen than on. Then there was Sir Miles and his wife. She's a bit intense and scraggy now, but you can still see she's been a beauty. Oh, and Evelyn Moorhouse—the Moorhouse heiress, you know. We and Roger were introduced, as a matter of fact. Let me see—why weren't you introduced, too, Hilma? Oh, of course. It was when you were having your dress put right. Pity. She's quite attractive. Didn't she get engaged some time ago? I've forgotten who the man was. No one important, if I remember rightly. Ah, well. I suppose if you're an heiress, you can marry for love."

"Come, Barbara, you aren't going to pretend that *you* did anything else, are you?" Hilma spoke smoothly and her smile held just the right degree of teasing amusement.

"Oh, well—no. Though I always tell Jim that if he'd been a thousand a year poorer he would just have missed the boat. After all, one must fix a limit."

"My *dear!* But one doesn't say so in so many words," protested her aunt with some delicacy—and some ingenuousness, Hilma thought.

"I do," Barbara said cheerfully. And Mrs. Arnall withdrew, faintly ruffled, from the argument.

"Can you come over on Sunday, Hilma? In the afternoon. There are quite a crowd of us going on afterwards to a cocktail party at the Burnthorpes. We'd like it if you'd come."

Barbara meant it. She was a generous-hearted young creature, and it gave her real pleasure to be able to include her cousin as much as possible in anything they were doing. She knew how circumstances had changed for the Arnalls, and she was among the few who had not cooled off just a little in consequence.

But this time Hilma shook her head.

"I'm so sorry, I'm afraid I can't on Sunday."

"Oh, were you going somewhere with Roger? You could bring him along, too, if you liked."

"No, I'm not going with Roger."

"Oh?" Barbara looked at her with frank inquisitiveness. She never demanded any privacy about her own actions, and was quite incapable of understanding why anyone else should wish for such a thing. The glance drew no information, however, and after a moment she said, "Well, never mind. Still, I'm sorry. The Moorhouse girl and her fiancé were coming. It would have given you a chance to meet her."

"Coming to *your* place, do you mean?" Hilma could not keep the astonished interest out of her voice.

"Oh, no, to the Burnthorpes' cocktail party afterwards."

"I see," Hilma said. But she was really thinking: "He *can't* be going to this wretched cocktail party if he's spending the afternoon with me at Richmond. Well, of course, he's not staying long. That's the explanation. He isn't 'spending the afternoon with me.' Just having a word or two. Much more sensible. It was silly of me to suggest anywhere so far out. That means he *can't* stay long, if he's to get back to Town, collect Evelyn and take her on to the cocktail party."

She found, to her surprise, that she was becoming quite accomplished at pursuing her own line of thought and yet managing to hold her place in a conversation. All the time Barbara's stream of chatter was running on she contrived to say just enough to keep it going, and yet was able to work out to herself just what would—or might—happen on Sunday.

When Barbara had gone, Mrs. Arnall said, quite innocently:

"Where *are* you going on Sunday, dear?"

It was unusual for her to make any enquiries about Hilma's activities, perhaps because she usually accepted the idea that Hilma was out with Roger. But in this case Hilma had owned quite specifically that she was not going with Roger, and, although Mrs. Arnall entertained no sort of suspicion, she did enquire quite casually where she *was* going.

Just for a second Hilma hesitated. Then she explained quite calmly and circumstantially that she was going to tea with some friend of hers of whom her mother knew, but with whom she was not actually acquainted.

Mrs. Arnall was perfectly satisfied, displayed no further curiosity, and the incident passed off. But Hilma hated the whole business suddenly.

One could not go on making appointments where one had to lie and deceive in order to keep them! That had never been in her scheme of things, and it made her feel strange and unhappy to be doing it now.

Not that there was any question of "going on making" such appointments. He must know that as well as she.

They had both enjoyed their unconventional little flutter of romance—had been prepared to end it with that single meeting. But for the dark background of the murder, the whole incident had been light, amusing, entirely insubstantial. To this day they were even ignorant of each other's names.

It had been really a little unfortunate that they should have met again—it gave a certain significance to the whole thing which neither of them would have been prepared to accord it. They were commonsense —even slightly cynical—people, who knew their world very well. They both had very definite schemes fort their future, and neither of them was likely to confuse the substance with the shadow.

Hilma felt better when she had worked all that out to herself. For five minutes she even convinced herself that it would be better not to keep the Sunday appointment, but simply to let the whole incident slip away into oblivion.

There was something a little cheap and foolish, however, in making an appointment and not keeping it. If she had had time to think, she would never have made it, of course, and no doubt he was reflecting on much the same lines by now. Still, the appointment *had* been made, and politeness and a certain cool common sense demanded that it should be kept. To break it ostentatiously would imply, for one thing, that it was a great deal more important than it was.

After all, presumably anyone could meet anyone in Richmond Park and go for a stroll on a Sunday afternoon. No one could pretend there was anything specially significant in that.

When Hilma reached the Robin Hood Gate on that Sunday afternoon, it seemed as though quite a number of people shared this view. Certainly there were plenty of them strolling about in the autumn sunshine. Children, couples, family parties—meeting, parting, talking, playing, flirting.

At first she thought: "Oh dear, I hadn't realised there would be so many people!" Then she reminded herself that solitude was hardly necessary for any interview they might have. Besides, further inside the Park one could find quiet and unfrequented ways.

She was a little early, the bus having taken less time than she had expected, but she had only been strolling up and down for a few minutes when she saw him coming.

He walked with a long, swinging, easy stride which she felt was characteristic, and she noticed that his slight, unselfconscious air of distinction made more than one person glance at him as he passed. He was entirely unaware of it, she saw, and the first time the settled gravity of his expression lifted was when his eyes lighted on her.

He smiled and came forward, raising his hat. And then she realised what it was that was faintly incongruous about this meeting. They were seeing each other by daylight for the first time. It gave a prosaic touch which had been lacking in their previous encounters, and she wondered a little how it would affect their attitude to each other.

He held her hand perhaps a fraction longer than was necessary as he greeted her. Then he said abruptly:

"I parked the car. I thought you would rather walk. But if you prefer driving, I can fetch it again in a few minutes."

"No, thank you, I'd rather walk," she told him. And then, a little curiously, she added, "I didn't know you had a car."

"Oh, yes." He had fallen into step beside her, and by common consent they turned down the path which offered most likelihood of solitude.

"What kind?" She was making polite conversation,

still very much aware of the bright October sunshine and the open air and the complete lack of fantasy about this meeting.

"E-type Jag."

"Oh, how nice." That was still polite conversation, but this time she thought: "Expensive tastes. Yes, he was right about having those. And there's nothing mass-production about that suit either."

Indeed she felt fairly certain that the light grey suit he was wearing had not been made more than half a mile from Savile Row.

"It was nice of you to come," he said suddenly. She noticed he no longer used the term "Liebling." Perhaps he, too, was aware that a sunny afternoon was not in keeping with the light, rather frothy little scenes which had taken place before.

"Well, it could hardly be a nicer afternoon for a walk, could it?" she smiled agreeably.

"No, it could hardly be a nicer afternoon," he agreed. "I suppose autumn and spring are your favourite times of the year?"

"Why?" She looked slightly surprised.

"Because they have that quality of faint melancholy which we once discussed, and which I think you said gave one a feeling of added tenderness towards things."

"Oh! Like Viennese—beauty," she said slowly.

"Yes, Liebling, like Viennese beauty."

He had said it! Quite simply. Quite naturally. And, strangely enough, it fitted the mood of the afternoon after all.

She thought deliberately: "We'll keep things on a prosaic level, though. As long as we keep the situation well in hand, we can say good-bye this afternoon without any unnecessary regrets."

Aloud, she said: "Do you know that you and I nearly met at a cocktail party this afternoon?"

"No, did we? How was that?"

"Well, you're going on to a cocktail party later, aren't you?"

"No," he said, "I'm not."

"Oh!" Hilma was faintly put out. "But I thought it was arranged. Weren't you going to the Burnthorpes' place?"

"No." He smiled slightly. "This arrangement was made first. By the time I heard of the other, my time was not free. I refused the invitation."

Hilma wondered a little how Evelyn took refusals of this sort. Somehow, although she had not seen much of the fiancée, she had an idea that she was not a girl who took "No" with a very good grace.

"You—could have fitted in both, I suppose." Hilma's tone was casual.

"I didn't think so," he said, and *his* tone was curt. She had the distinct impression that there had been just a little unpleasantness about the discussion with Evelyn. In a way, that was all to the good. It would mean that he was beginning to realise, as well as she herself, that this friendship of theirs was ill-judged—impossible to pursue beyond the very restricted limits it had already reached.

It was not that it was dangerous. "Dangerous" was too big a word with which to dignify it. It was ill-judged. That was the exact expression. It cut across their other, and *really* important, concerns, and, as such, must be dismissed. They would part quite good friends, of course—smilingly, a little regretfully. But there it was.

She was pretty sure, from his abstracted air, that he had worked things out to much the same conclusion.

"So you know the Burnthorpes, too?" He spoke at last, breaking quite a long silence.

"Well, no, as a matter of fact, I don't know them. They're friends of a cousin of mine. My cousin wanted me and—and Roger to go there this afternoon, and then accompany her and her husband to the cocktail party."

"All without masks this time, eh?" He looked reflectively ahead, and his smile was a little complicated. "That would have been rather a tangling of the threads, wouldn't it?"

"Yes, that was how it struck me. Made me think that—it was time——" She hesitated diplomatically.

"Time we said, '*Addio, senza rancor*'?" he suggested.

"Which means?"

"More or less, 'Good-bye, without any bad feeling on either side.' But, used in its context—it's from *Bohème*, you know—it rather implies, 'Good-bye, while there's still time to do it without regrets on either side.' "

"Very well expressed." Hilma's cool little laugh applauded the sentiment even more than her comment did.

"Shall we sit down here?" He spoke abruptly again, indicating a bench where sunshine and shadow cast a perpetually moving pattern.

She agreed at once. She felt that the right atmosphere had certainly been achieved. Even quite a long conversation now would be harmless. It might even be amusing. For there was no question but that they did share the same sense of humour.

"It's nice here." She carelessly pulled off her gloves, and immediately his attention was attracted by her engagement ring.

"Hm-hm, very fine." A little mockingly he took her hand in his and examined the ring.

"Didn't you see it the other night—at the ball?"

"I was not looking at your hands then," he said dryly.

She had some difficulty in finding an immediate answer to that, and in the pause he observed, with his eyes still on the ring:

"A very handsome piece of evidence of a very satisfactory state of affairs."

"I think so, too," she agreed coolly. "By the way, I thought—your Evelyn very charming when I identified her the other evening."

"Oh, she is."

"Are you thinking of getting married pretty soon?" Her attention seemed at least half-absorbed by an adventurous bird which was hopping nearer and nearer to where they were sitting.

There was a queer little pause. Then he said:

"Probably just after Christmas. Evelyn fancies a Riviera honeymoon, so we should probably combine it with an escape from the worst of a London winter."

"It's a good idea," Hilma agreed.

"And you?"

"Much about the same time, I think. My brother should be home by then. He's in America on business at the moment. I should like him to be home for my wedding."

"Of course." He was politely interested. "Your only brother?"

"Hm-hm. We were always great friends as children."

He smiled at her then, quite deliberately.

"What a nice child you must have been, Liebling. Bright blue eyes and, I suppose, about half a yard of golden hair hanging down your back."

Hilma laughed.

"I had long hair, certainly. I don't know about being a 'nice child.' I think Tony and I were exceptionally naughty in some things. That—penknife was his," she added irrelevantly.

"Which? Oh, the one you used for burgling my flat?"

"If you must put it that way," she smiled demurely, "yes."

"What a very shocking use for a memento of innocent childhood," he remarked mockingly.

"Tony wouldn't have thought so," she retorted quickly. "We used it for opening windows before now."

"Dear me! Did you make a joint concern of other burgling escapades?"

"Oh, no. But when we stayed on my grandfather's farm, we used to slip out at night by our window, slide down the roof of a shed, and go off to enjoy the moonlight. Then we had to get in again by the kitchen window and creep up the back stairs. We used the knife for opening the window."

"Hence the experienced touch with which you broke into my flat?"

"I'm afraid so."

He looked at her—smilingly, reflectively, just a little too admiringly, considering the excellent remarks which had been made about saying good-bye.

"It seems rather an incongruous beginning for the golden girl you were to become."

"I wonder," Hilma said a little doubtfully, "in just what sense you mean that expression."

" 'Golden girl'? Every sense. It's how I always think of you. Your wonderful hair, your expensive outlook, your exquisite air which always suggests that the best is only just good enough."

"Oh." She was busy digesting this statement when a very fat little boy in a very tight suit approached them and said:

"Please c'n you tell me the time?"

"Nothing like tea-time yet."

"Oh, *dear*!"

"Five past four. Is that any good to you?"

The little boy shook his head.

"Tea isn't until five."

"Hard lines. What have you got tucked away there under your arm?"

"My wagon. It's broken. The wheel's come off." Life was altogether a stale and profitless business, it seemed.

"Give it here to me. I'll see if I can mend it."

Hilma was a good deal amused at her companion's sure handling of the situation. Neither he nor the little boy took much notice of her in this man-to-man discussion. They both bent over the broken wagon.

"Can you do it?" the little boy enquired anxiously.

"I think so, if you don't breathe all over it like that."

The child straightened up.

"I'm very tired," he said pointedly. "I've been walking miles."

"Pioneer, eh? You'd better sit down."

The little boy made a not very successful attempt to scramble on to the rather high seat and then Hilma was still further amused to see the expert way his plump little figure was lifted on to the seat between.

"There you are. Now you sit very quiet while I finish this."

The child slowly rubbed his hands over his knees. Then he looked at Hilma, apparently noticing her for the first time, and enquired sociably:

"Is he your husband?"

"No."

The knees were rubbed a bit more.

"He's very clever, isn't he?"

Hilma laughed.

"She can't tell you, old chap. She doesn't know me well enough. And I haven't mended any of *her* toys."

The little boy thought that funny and laughed. Then he leant over to see how the wagon was getting on.

"Is it nearly finished?" He leant confidingly against the arm next to him.

"Very nearly."

"I think you're very clever, even if she doesn't."

"Thanks, I'm flattered. There you are." The wagon was set on the ground, pushed backwards and forwards once or twice and pronounced satisfactory by its critical owner.

"I s'pose I've got to go now."

"Well, we don't insist, do we, Liebling?"

Hilma shook her head.

"*What's* her name?" The little boy seemed surprised at the form of address.

"Liebling," was the grave reply, though the dark eyes sparkled amusedly.

The little boy shook his head slowly.

"It's a funny name," he remarked.

"Think so? I rather thought it suited her."

Hilma moved slightly, perhaps in protest. But the child was not specially interested in that aspect of things. He said firmly:

"*My* name's Richard."

"A very excellent and romantic-sounding name."

"What's romantic?"

"Ah! Now you're posing one of those questions that

people find exceedingly difficult to answer. What *is* 'romantic,' Liebling?" Those laughing eyes were turned on her now, though he went on almost immediately: "I suppose one might call it the gilt on the gingerbread, Richard, or the glitter that makes one think things are gold when they are not."

"It sounds silly," remarked the puzzled Richard somewhat crushingly, whereat Hilma gave a short laugh, and her companion said:

"Do you know, I'm very much afraid you've said the last—and wisest—word on the subject. It is silly. Or rather, it belongs to those charming, foolish things for which there is no room at all in everyday life. Isn't that right, Liebling?"

"Perfectly right," Hilma agreed coolly. "I think one could hardly put it better."

"Is it nearly tea-time now?" The little boy found this conversation dull—not to say foolish—and his thoughts turned to more congenial subjects once more.

Hilma glanced at her watch this time, laughed sympathetically, and said, "I'm afraid not."

But her companion had better ideas. Putting his hand into his pocket, he produced some coins, which he studied thoughtfully.

"I think, though, it might be time for lemonade," he remarked reflectively.

"From the man with the sweet stall?" Richard found this much more interesting and to the point than a discussion on romance.

"Yes, from the man with the sweet stall. That is, if he sells it?"

"Oh, yes. In big jars with a lemon stuck on top." Richard seemed an authority on the subject.

"I know. Bright yellow stuff. Extremely unwholesome, no doubt, but very palatable when one is under seven. Well, here you are." Money was handed over and eagerly clutched in a fat, hot hand. "Run along and have your lemonade. And then by the time you've dragged your wagon home, it will probably be tea-time."

The little boy seemed to think so, too. He viewed the whole transaction with marked approval and then scrambled down with a breathless "Thank you."

"Good-bye," He shook hands politely with his benefactor. "Thank you for mending my wagon. Good-bye, Leebing." He shook hands too with Hilma, who smiled and expressed the hope that he would enjoy his lemonade.

"Oh, yes, I shall," he assured her as he trundled off with his wagon. "I'm so glad I met you."

When he had gone, Hilma turned to her companion with a laugh.

"He was rather sweet, wasn't he?"

"Very."

"You seem to know quite a lot about children."

"Oh—no." He looked surprised. "Do I? Why?"

"Well, you handled him in a very expert way, and were not at all self-conscious. Most unmarried men are a bit—unless they happen to know a good deal about children."

"I'm not sure that I know much about them." He smiled slightly. "But I like children very much."

"Do you?"

"Does that surprise you so much?"

"We-ell, a little, I think. It doesn't somehow fit in with the rest of you."

"Not part of the make-up of a second-rate character?" he suggested.

Hilma laughed.

"Something like that, I suppose. Still"—she gave a rather mocking little inclination of her head—"it's nice to know you'll make a good husband and father."

"Eh?" He looked faintly startled. "Oh, yes—of course. Didn't you say once that something like that was part of your attraction for Roger? That you would make a good wife and mother, I mean?"

"Did I? Yes, I daresay." She looked reflective. "Funny, isn't it, that you and I, of all people, are going to have thrust upon us the rôle of very solid, worthwhile people. All the standard virtues, I mean, and none of the pleasant, inconsequential frivolities which really come more naturally to us."

He looked at her very thoughtfully.

"Yes, I know what you mean." Then, after a slight pause: "Do you object to the rôle very much?"

"Excellent wife and mother? It isn't much good objecting, is it?"

"I didn't ask you that." He was serious and there was a touch of something like obstinacy about him. "I asked how you would like it."

Her rather easy smile faded curiously.

"We're being quite serious now?"

"Quite serious."

"Well—I think—yes. I should like to have children. One child, anyway."

"Roger's child." He didn't look at her that time, and there was a queer moment of silence.

Then, when she answered, her voice was cool and toneless.

"Circumstances being what they are—Roger's, naturally."

There was a slight pause again. Then she said more lightly:

"And you? How will you fancy the rôle of parent?"

He looked away across the Park, smiling slightly.

"I should like to have something rather like our little fat friend of the wagon."

Hilma laughed, though, for some unknown reason, she was rather touched by the way he said that.

"Well, I daresay you will."

He shook his head.

"Not?" She was surprised. "But surely—do you mean that Evelyn doesn't want——" Hilma stopped. "Oh, really, I'm sorry. It's hardly my business, of course."

He shrugged, and again there was that faint smile.

"It doesn't matter. We haven't observed so many restrictions in our previous conversations, you and I, that we need begin now. Anyway, I didn't mean that. I think Evelyn is quite—keen on children. At least—shall I say?—she counts them in the scheme of things."

"Then what—did you mean quite by saying you were not likely to have any—any nice fat little boys like that one?"

He didn't answer that directly.

"Did you notice," he said, "that he had very fair hair and blue eyes?"

"Why, yes, I think I did. Yes, of course I did." A faint uneasiness stirred in her heart—a sort of anticipation of something that might hurt.

"Well, if romantic fancy were to be indulged—that is how I would like any child of mine to be. Fair hair and blue eyes."

There was a profound silence. Then, with an effort, Hilma laughed.

"Too bad! Evelyn is as dark as you are, isn't she?"

"Yes."

"Well, anyway, it's only—only romantic fancy, as you say. I thought you meant something serious."

For a moment she saw his nostrils distend slightly. Then quite deliberately he matched his mood with hers.

"Oh, forgive me for giving the wrong impression, Liebling." He laughed in his turn. "We never mean anything quite seriously, you and I, do we? How foolish of me to put it so gravely. All romantic fancy—nothing else. It's just human nature to hanker after what one can't have."

Hilma nodded and answered quite gaily.

"True enough! As things are, it's *I* who will probably have the blue-eyed little blondes, while all the time, now I come to think of it, I'm perverse enough to feel that I'd much prefer a little boy with big dark eyes and solemn ways and——" But she could not complete it after all. To her own utter astonishment, she quite suddenly put her face in her hands.

"Don't, Liebling."

The tone was soft but urgent. She thought perhaps he too could not have borne to have that sentence gaily completed.

She hardly knew what she expected him to do next. How could she, when she could not even account for her own action? Incoherently she kept on repeating to herself: "It's absurd. I don't even know his name."

Then one of her hands was taken away from her face, and held very tightly in his. Still he said nothing, and when she looked up determinedly a moment later, he was very pale and a trifle grim. She felt she must be looking white, too, and certainly his expression softened as his eyes rested on her.

"I am sorry, Liebling. We should never have started the subject. It was my fault."

"No." She gave a shaky little laugh. "Shall we say it

was Richard's fault? He—he rather made one's thoughts—— Well, anyway, it doesn't matter. We've said a great deal too much already, haven't we? Indulging our—our romantic fancy, or whatever it is."

He nodded.

"You're right, of course. Rotten world, isn't it, Liebling?"

"Or else we're rather rotten people?"

"Wanting to eat our cake and have it, you mean? Yes, I suppose that's it. What a pity we aren't heroic and determined and the possessors of lots of stern character." He was half laughing again.

"Or else that we didn't know just how ghastly life can be without the particular things we want." She said that almost crisply. Perhaps because something still hurt. Perhaps because she was realising just how far they had come from the excellent common-sense basis they had established at the beginning of their conversation.

"It isn't only moonlight and the late hours that can be dangerous," Hilma told herself grimly. "Sunshine and Richmond Park can be just as bad." And then, with a coolness which she knew was her best defence, she said:

"Even if you're not going to that cocktail party, I'm afraid I have to go. I—didn't mean to stay so late, in any case."

For a moment she saw startled protest in his eyes. Then he too became cool and matter-of-fact.

"Very well. Can I run you back to Town?" He got up and stood there looking down at her—calm, polite, imperturbable.

"No, really, thanks, but there's no need."

"It would be a pleasure."

"A pleasure," Hilma said deliberately, "in which it would be much wiser not to indulge."

Again there was that expression of startled protest—to be replaced almost immediately by a cool acceptance of facts.

"As you like, of course." He bowed slightly to her.

She wanted to say angrily that it was not at all as she liked, and that he knew it, and that she didn't suppose it was as *he* liked either, only what could one do?

But naturally she said none of these things. They would only have led to stormy discussion that would have ended in—Heaven knew what. The one essential of the moment was that they should remain calm and collected, free from any sort of heat or emotion, satisfied to accept the inescapable fact that, in this world, one cannot have everything. Only one must know *what* one wanted, and hold to that in the face of any sort of romantic temptation to make a fool of oneself.

"I think"— she looked up at him determinedly —"I'll say good-bye to you now, and I'll stay here a little longer while—while you go."

"But you forget"—he smiled at her very gently, perhaps because he admired her courage—"that it was you who had to go. I'm in no hurry. Let's say good-bye here, as you suggest, but you will go and I shall stay here."

She thought he was simply making difficulties and shrugged impatiently.

"Very well." She got to her feet, too, then, and held out her hand.

He took both her hands, however, and smiled straight at her.

"Good-bye, Liebling. It's been—wonderful," he

said, and, bending his head, he kissed first one hand and then the other.

She wished she could have kissed him then, and her fingers curled tightly round his in the effort of keeping herself from doing so. For she *had* to make that effort. It was too late now for anything like that. The break had already been made, and it would have been madness to ignore it.

"Good-bye." Hilma spoke very softly in her turn. "I—I hope you're awfully happy."

"My dear, hope you are, too."

She had drawn her hands away and turned from him almost before she knew what she was doing. And she was walking along the path, out of his life.

Only then did she realise why it was he had made her go while he stayed. Not to make difficulties, as she had supposed, but to make things easier for her. For it must be easier, surely, to walk on and on—to *do* something—than to wait, watching someone walk out of your life and make no protest.

"I could have done it if I'd *had* to," Hilma told herself fiercely. But she was glad it had not been her part to wait.

## CHAPTER SIX

LONG before Hilma reached home again, she had entirely recovered her self-control. She was even slightly surprised at herself for having momentarily lost it. It was not as though she were a girl who had ever been in much doubt about what she wanted—at least, not of late years.

Roger had not been the only man who had wanted to marry her—but he had been very much the most desirable match. And, in the ordinary way, it was not even necessary for her to enumerate the advantages to herself. They were self-evident.

Rich, devoted, indulgent and a thoroughly good sort. What more could one ask of any prospective husband?

"And I'm fond of him," Hilma told herself—firmly and, as a matter of fact, quite truthfully. "I'm fond of him in that sensible, solid, day-to-day fashion which makes such a good basis for marriage. I know quite well, of course, what it is that I feel I'm missing." She was determinedly honest with herself, because she prided herself on always facing facts. "It's the lovely, gay, unreasoning romance that one dreams of as a girl."

But could she really pretend to herself, in the light of cold experience, that such romance often came one's way? Or if it did, how often did it outlast the more tangible advantages of a "sensible" marriage?

"A pity—but there it is," reflected Hilma with a rueful little smile. "One of the advantages—or disadvantages—of having a clear-cut outlook is that you can't trick yourself into enjoying the risks of the unknown instead of feeling the comfort of solid ground beneath your feet."

And as she turned in at the gate of the indefinably shoddy house where she and her parents now lived, she thought almost fiercely of all the pleasant things which the "solid ground" of her future with Roger implied.

"Is that you, Hilma dear?" her mother called from the drawing-room. "Here is Aunt Mary come to see us."

The brightness of Mrs. Arnall's tone might have

given the impression that a visit from Aunt Mary was an unexpected pleasure. In actual fact it was merely unexpected. "Aunt Mary" was Hilma's great-aunt, a fearsome and unlovable old lady whose favourite remark was: "I always let all my relations know that my dear husband left me only a life interest in his money, and that after my death it will go to charity. Then they have no reason to wish me dead."

It had never, apparently, occurred to her that there might be other—and even more pressing—reasons for such uncharitable thoughts to pass through the minds of her relations.

Towards her great-niece, however, she had been known to unbend occasionally. And, as Hilma came into the room now, she received a bright stare of interest and a rather wintry smile.

"How d'you do, Hilma. Dear me, child, what a colour you've got! Anyone can see you've been out with your sweetheart," was her somewhat unfortunate opening.

Mrs. Arnall coughed embarrassedly, but Hilma laughed as she bent to kiss Aunt Mary's cheek, presented for that purpose.

"You look well, too, Aunt Mary."

"I'm not at all well," snapped Aunt Mary. "In fact, I've been very poorly indeed, only I don't make a fuss about it like a lot of people, and so no one bothers to notice. You've grown since I last saw you."

Hilma knew it was useless to point out how extremely improbable this was at twenty-five, so she compromised diplomatically with:

"I expect it's because I have on higher heels today."

Aunt Mary inspected her heels and said:

"Possibly. They certainly seem a very ridiculous

height to me," which was the nearest she could bring herself to agreeing with anyone.

Mrs. Arnall appeared to feel that an amiable diversion was necessary, for she remarked with a slightly strained smile:

"Aunt Mary has some *very* nice news for you, Hilma."

"Thank you, Cecily," cut in Aunt Mary sharply. "I'm perfectly capable of explaining myself without your assistance."

Mrs. Arnall relapsed into silence.

"So you're getting married quite soon?" Aunt Mary transferred her remarkably bright gaze to Hilma.

"I expect so," Hilma agreed.

"What do you mean, you expect so? Doesn't he want you, after all?"

"Oh, *yes*!" Hilma laughed. "I only meant that we hadn't fixed the date of the wedding yet."

"Well, it's time you did," Aunt Mary said. "Too long engagements are just as dangerous as too short ones. People get restless. Anyway, I've been talking to your mother about your trousseau. She and your father can't do much about sending you to your husband decently dressed, of course. So I'm going to see about it."

"Aunt Mary!" Hilma was divided between astonishment at this unusual generosity and resentment at the offensive way of putting it. "I—don't know—what to say."

"There's no need to say anything except 'Thank you.' I'm not a rich woman," stated Aunt Mary incorrectly, "but I'm willing to give you a cheque for five hundred pounds. You should be able to buy an adequate trousseau for that."

"Adequate! Why, Aunt Mary, it's a fortune! I——"

"It's nothing of the sort," retorted Aunt Mary, exceedingly pleased. "But it should suffice."

"It's wonderfully generous of you. I can't possibly thank you enough," Hilma said earnestly.

"We-ell——" For once Aunt Mary left a statement unchallenged. "I won't say that I should have done it in all circumstances. But I don't mind telling you, Hilma, I'm very pleased about this marriage of yours."

Hilma smiled, wondering just a little why Aunt Mary should be pleased. However, the old lady was not inclined to leave herself unexplained, and she went on at once:

"It's what I call a really sensible marriage. You're quite a pretty girl in your way, Hilma, and I dare say a lot of silly young men talk nonsense to you. But I'm glad to see you chose someone in a solid and reliable position, someone who could support you decently. I approve of common sense, and I'm quite willing to show my approval this way. I shouldn't have given you *anything* if you had been marrying some penniless young flibbertigibbet just because he looked like your favourite pop star."

"But, Aunt Mary," Hilma was genuinely amused, "you could never have supposed I should marry for such a reason."

"No," the old lady admitted. "No, I can't say I really expected you to be *so* silly, but one never knows with girls. Some silly little flutter of romance—and there they are, ready to throw away goodness knows what for a few cheap thrills."

Hilma deliberately switched her mind away from certain happenings of the last week or two.

"Sacrificing the substance for the shadow, in fact?" she suggested.

"Exactly. Though I object to clichés," retorted Aunt Mary tartly.

"Well, as you see"— Hilma spoke just a trifle dryly —"I exercised the common sense you so much admire, Aunt Mary, and chose to marry someone in what you call a solid and reliable position."

"Quite so. And that's why I am going to give you your trousseau," agreed her great-aunt, who was evidently a firm supporter of the view that "to him who hath shall be given."

"Isn't it lovely, dear?" Mrs. Arnall smiled at her daughter. Not all the sharpness of Aunt Mary's conversation could cloud her relief and pleasure at the actual offer.

"Lovely," Hilma agreed, and felt an unaccustomed lump in her throat. She was not quite sure if it was for her mother or because of something quite vague and inexplicable which had nothing to do with trousseau or Aunt Mary.

Aunt Mary was a woman of decided action. She also had a distinct weakness for drama. So that, before she left the house, she slowly wrote out a cheque for Hilma, repeating carefully, as she did so, "Five hundred pounds," just in case Hilma or her mother should have failed to appreciate the extraordinary extent of her generosity.

"Thank you, Aunt Mary, very, very much indeed." Hilma stood there, twisting the little pink slip of paper in her hand. "I do appreciate it, you know."

"Well, I hope so," Aunt Mary said. "Now don't run away with the idea that I shall come to your rescue again in every crisis. It won't be any good running up debts and then coming to me instead of to your husband."

Hilma could not imagine anything that she was less

ikely to do, but she murmured submissively, "No, Aunt Mary."

"And I hope, Hilma, that when you have your first daughter, you will remember the one relation who has been generous to you."

Hilma managed to make some tactfully noncommittal reply. Then she summoned the taxi which her great-aunt requested, and dutiffuly saw her into it.

After Aunt Mary's providential generosity there was, as Mrs. Arnall remarked, no real reason to prolong the engagement much further. She seemed to imagine the whole problem looming much larger in Hilma's mind than had really been the case.

"Oh, I know how you were feeling, dear," she assured Hilma sympathetically. "There was always that horrid knowledge that your trousseau did present a very real problem. Not that Roger really minds what you wear, of course," she added in hasty justice to Roger. "But any girl wants *some* nice clothes when she gets married. And each time you thought of fixing a date for your wedding you must have wondered what we were going to do about your outfit. Oh, I noticed. I knew you were restless and worried, even though you said nothing."

Hilma smiled and allowed her mother to retain her own theories. It was impossible to tell her that any restlessness had had nothing whatever to do with anxiety about her trousseau. Nor had Roger entered into it in the slightest degree.

But certainly the munificent cheque did solve a great many problems. And, with a curious feeling that she was thereby erecting some sort of safety barrier round herself, Hilma began to make plans for spending some of the money.

Roger was undisguisedly pleased at these signs of interest on her part.

"I think, Hilma," he said, with an air of having given the matter much consideration, "it would be a good idea to plan our wedding for just after Christmas. And then we might have a Riviera honeymoon and escape the worst of the winter here."

He was so obviously delighted with the scheme he had thought out that Hilma had to conceal her dismay and her ironical amusement with the utmost care. To think that he should actually have chosen the same honeymoon as——

Oh, well, it was ridiculous to mind, of course. Surely the Riviera was large enough to hold two honeymoon couples without their having to meet. But there *was* something quite uncanny about the association of ideas.

"Well, Hilma? What do you think of it?" Roger was a very good-tempered man, but he liked the applause to follow pretty quickly when he propounded a good idea.

"It would—be lovely." Hilma hesitated. "But I had rather thought—what about Italy? I should love to go there."

"I don't care much for the Italians," stated Roger, who was somewhat given to these large and quite unqualified statements.

Hilma was sorely tempted for a moment to point out that, as he was an extremely insular person, perhaps he would not like the French any better. However, knowing quite well that his reply would be a tolerant, "Well, of course, they're all foreigners, anyway," she refrained from pursuing the subject.

"Let's think it over a bit," she suggested. And Roger rather reluctantly agreed to this, although he obviously thought that full consideration *had* been given to the subject already.

Mrs. Arnall, too, was very happy in these days of

wedding preparations. Hilma reflected, not without a certain touch of humour, that quite a lot of people were getting more enjoyment out of her approaching marriage than perhaps she was herself.

There was Aunt Mary, with the pleasant certainty that only her cheque had saved the whole thing from being a pretty shabby affair. There was her mother, delighthing in spending money quite lavishly for once—even if it was not upon herself. And there was Roger, contentedly aware that the best idea he had ever had was about to be put into actual practice.

Even her father said: "Well, my dear, I'm very glad to think you'll soon be setting up house on your own in such fine style. You're one of those people to whom money is very becoming, Hilma."

"Isn't it becoming to all of us?" asked Hilma with a smile. But her father shook his head.

"No, it's like a dress suit to some men. They simply shouldn't wear it. But you—well, you'll 'wear' money very attractively, my dear."

"Yes, I know what you mean, of course. I suppose that's why I—why I attach a good deal of importance to the things money can buy. Not just the material, tangible things. Security and freedom to enjoy art and the power to live a gracious existence and—and—oh, all that sort of thing."

Her father nodded.

"Quite right, my dear. That's what I look forward to when I make my pile again. And you know, I don't think that day is so far off, Hilma." He smiled reflectively into the fire. "Of course I haven't said anything to your mother yet, because she's a little pessimistic in these matters. But I must say there are some very interesting things happening in the City these days. Things that a man of foresight and knowledge can turn to his own account."

"I'm sure of it, Father." Hilma smiled at him rather sadly. But he was quite unaware of that because he was looking into the fire, where he saw reflected golden dreams of the future.

Sometimes Hilma wondered a little if she had dreamt that queer, moving interlude with the man who called her "Liebling." And then she would find that just the repetition of the word brought him so clearly before her that he could not have been a figure in any dream. She could see him exactly—in the sunlight as he sat mending Richard's wagon in Richmond Park—in the moonlight that night in the garden as he took off his mask and smiled at her with those faintly cynical eyes—in the flat as he stood in the doorway, grimly watching her rifle his desk.

Besides, he was inextricably mixed up with the death of Charles Martin and the end of that sordid threat of blackmail. There was no dream about that. She was free! Absolutely and blessedly free—to go on with her marriage to Roger.

It was about the middle of November that Hilma received the letter. Not a specially significant-looking letter, but she glanced at the envelope with a certain amount of interest because the writing was quite unknown to her.

Her mother had brought it in, together with a postcard about an appointment for fitting some of Hilma's dresses. This was of great interest to Mrs. Arnall and occasioned a whole stream of comment and question.

Hilma slit open the envelope and drew out the single sheet of thick cream notepaper.

"Liebling," the letter began.

Somehow she concealed the start which she gave—even contrived to answer her mother coherently, while she pretended to glance, idly through the letter.

But she knew she must not read it in front of her mother. She must get away somewhere where she could read it alone.

"So you see, dear," her mother's voice ran on, "it would be *much* better for you to make some sort of decision about it now——"

Hilma wondered absently what she was talking about, but she said thoughtfully:

"Yes, you're quite right, of course. I'll think it over carefully, and really make up my mind."

"I should." Mrs. Arnall looked pleased, and certainly took no notice of the fact that Hilma pushed her letter into the pocket of her suit, practically unread, as she went out of the room.

Upstairs in her bedroom, Hilma sat down on the side of her bed and drew out the letter again.

"*Liebling*." Even at that moment it amused and half pleased her that he still called her that, although he must know her name now. *"As we agreed that I should look at your name and address for only one reason, you will understand why it is that I am writing to you. Evelyn's very tiresome and somewhat superfluous cousin has returned from America, and seems more than a little inclined to make trouble.*

*"I shall be having tea at Jerringham's in New Bond Street about four-thirty to-morrow. Should you happen to come in then, need I say that I shall be delighted to see you? Auf Wiedersehen."*

It was not even signed, and that fact made Hilma smile dryly in spite of everything. Perhaps he thought she was a little too careless with compromising letters to be trusted with his name. She supposed, as she sat there twisting the letter in her hands, that she could hardly blame him.

Dismay was the principal feeling in her heart, she assured herself. Dismay that the ground could have opened under their feet again like this. Oh, why did one indiscretion always lead to another? This wretched cousin could make any amount of trouble—not only with that other magnificent engagement, but with her own! One could never tell how far the repercussions would reach. She had been building so securely during the last few weeks, and now——

Her eyes went back to the letter. Jerringham's in New Bond Street about four-thirty to-morrow. That was the rendezvous. And she found suddenly that the dismay was not so deep as it should have been, and there was a feeling of nervous excitement which had nothing to do with the trouble which the cousin might make.

Well, there was no harm, of course, in seeing him on something which was strictly business. A pity that they had to meet again—even a little unsettling, but she could hardly allow this wonderful engagement of his to go on the rocks for want of a few words of explanation from herself.

She would keep this appointment to-morrow, hear what it was that he wanted her to do, and then feel comfortably certain that *this* time at least they could lay all the ghosts of past indiscretions.

Jerringham's in New Bond Street is not a large place, but the spacing of the tables and the discretion of the lighting give one an impression of privacy and seclusion that is very acceptable when one is conducting delicate conversation. Hilma recognised at once that he had chosen well as she entered the place the following afternoon. Anyone might run into an acquaintance quite casually there and, having done so, would undoubtedly settle down to talk in this pleasant atmosphere.

His air of pleased surprise as he rose to meet her was admirable, and she thought from the sparkle in his eyes that he rather enjoyed giving an artistically complete impression of the rôle he was playing.

"This is delightful. Please do join me, won't you? Or are you expecting someone else?"

"Don't be ridiculous," whispered Hilma as he took her coat, but she rather wished that Roger would sometimes do nice, silly things like this.

They sat down opposite each other, and she glanced at him quickly to see if he bore any signs of marked anxiety about the dilemma in which he found himself. She could not discover any, but decided that he would be unlikely to show concern in any case.

They talked trivialities until tea had been brought. Then, as she began to pour out, Hilma said:

"Well, what is the position? Serious?"

"At the moment, yes. He is under the impression that one of my weaknesses is to entertain lovely ladies in my flat with considerable regularity, but at most irregular hours."

"Feels it his duty to save his cousin from a penniless adventurer, in fact?" suggested Hilma.

"Oh—well, rather more than that. If that were the only charge, I suppose I shouldn't have a leg to stand on."

"What do you mean?" Hilma looked startled.

"Why, Liebling"—he smiled straight into her eyes, as he took his tea from her—"what else would you call me?"

She bit her lip slightly. Then she said:

"All right, we'll let that pass."

He laughed.

"We both are, you know," he reminded her teasingly. "Oh, very charming adventurers, of course, but"—he smiled regretfully—"adventurers."

Hilma's reluctant little laugh gave something like assent to that, though she thought she would rather like to have argued with him the subtle distinction between exploiting someone and giving them value for their beastly money.

"Well, anyway, that's beside the point," she said a little hastily. He was gravely attentive at once, though there was still something rather teasing about him. "I suppose he read the worst into our—our supper party?"

"He read into it exactly what we told the police sergeant, I'm afraid."

"Oh, yes, of course. I forgot that we piled up the evidence against ourselves."

"Yes. It seems to me now that I added several artistic details that were hardly necessary, though at the time they seemed admirable," he admitted.

"Well, there wasn't much time to think things out, was there?"

He shook his head, and they both smiled slightly, to remember the adventure they had shared together.

"Briefly, it comes to this, Liebling." He roused himself to more practical matters. "He challenged me with having someone in my flat for—shall we call it?—a disreputable purpose. I told him that if he would give me a day or two to find my proof I could satisfy him entirely, and he reluctantly agreed to keep his information to himself for the time being."

"I see. Now it's up to me to give him a convincing account of what I was really doing." He frowned, but she ignored that and went on determinedly: "Of course, there's no actual proof—he'll have to accept my word for it—but I think I can convince him that I'm not quite the type of young woman he imagines."

"I don't like the business at all." The interruption came almost violently. "I don't know what I was thinking of to suppose that I could let you go and tell that fool all about your private affairs."

"Don't be silly." Hilma was perfectly cool. "We've been over all this before. It wouldn't be any more than a momentary embarrassment for me. I don't know him. I'm never particularly likely to see him again. What is that measured against the wreck of your marriage? You aren't much of an adventurer, when it comes to the point, you know," she added with a smile.

He smiled too, but reluctantly.

"There ought to be *some* way out of it without dragging you in," he declared impatiently.

"Well, there isn't." Hilma was firm. "Besides, I'm not being dragged in. If you remember, I forced my way in, in the most unmistakable manner. That's what the whole trouble is about. It would be too absurdly quixotic of you to allow yourself to be compromised, simply because some girl, whose name you don't even know, broke into your flat by mistake."

He smiled again—not at all reluctantly that time, but brilliantly, with all his admiration in his eyes.

"I do know your name now. It's a lovely name—Hilma."

She laughed.

"It has a sort of Scandinavian sound that suits my colouring, I suppose. That's why people usually like it."

"Yes, it suits you. But 'Liebling' suits you better. Hilma is Scandinavian, as you say, and a little—cold."

"I'm rather cold by temperament," Hilma assured him calmly.

"No, Liebling, not by temperament. By force of circumstances, perhaps. But that's a very different thing."

"Well, we didn't come here to discuss temperaments." She said that much more sharply than she meant to, and he immediately leant his elbows on the table and smiled at her coaxingly.

"But it's a very interesting subject to discuss, don't you think?"

She refused to be drawn, however.

"Perhaps so. But we were going to arrange about my meeting Evelyn's cousin."

"No, we weren't," he retorted obstinately. "We were discussing whether it was necessary for you to meet him at all."

"But if there's any doubt about the matter, where's the sense in *our* meeting like this? Your sole reason for asking me here was to arrange about meeting the cousin, I suppose."

"No, it wasn't." He thrust his hands into his pockets and looked boyishly sulky. "It was a heaven-sent opportunity for seeing you again."

She felt her heart melt so absurdly at that expression of his that she had to make an effort to speak as dryly as the occasion demanded.

"If you got me here on false pretences, I think there's no point in my staying. And that means you cheated over the name and address, too," she pointed out curtly.

"Liebling!" He looked genuinely startled. "I must have made you very angry for you to speak like that."

"No." She spoke more gently that time, because her control was slipping a little. "No, not very angry. A little angry, because I don't like cheating."

"It wasn't cheating, really," he pleaded softly. "I did imagine we should arrange something—only I was happy, too, that I had to see you. Now I begin to have misgivings again about your seeing the cousin."

"Well"—she very lightly touched the hand that was resting on the table now—"you'll have to banish the misgivings, because I'm quite determined to see this cousin. What's his name, by the way? We can't go on calling him 'the Cousin,' like a character in a melodrama."

"Moorhouse. The same as Evelyn's name. And it *is* slightly like a melodrama, isn't it?" he smiled at her.

"Is it?" She considered that thoughtfully. "Yes, I suppose so. Blackmail, murder—and a couple of adventurers. Dear me, how horrified Roger would, be if he could hear that."

"He hasn't a great sense of humour, our friend Roger?"

"No," Hilma said. "No, Roger's worst enemy couldn't accuse him of having a sense of humour."

"*You* have a great sense of humour, Liebling."

"Well, no doubt I'll get over it," Hilma told him dryly. "In five years' time I daresay I shall wonder what I found funny in half the things we laugh over."

"Or perhaps you will even have forgotten they happened—in five years' time."

"Perhaps," Hilma said. And then, because she had a great reluctance to pursue that subject, she added almost at once: "Do you suppose we could go along and see this Mr. Moorhouse now?"

"At his flat?"

"Um-hm. Do you think he would be in?"

"I could ring up and enquire."

"Well, I think that would be a good idea, don't you?"

"If you're quite determined to tell him your story."

"Quite determined," she smiled firmly.

He got up then, and stood for a moment looking down at her.

"Tell me quite truthfully, do you hate it very much?"

She laughed and gave a slight shrug.

"I have enjoyed other things more. But I imagine that this too will be forgotten—in five years' time."

He didn't say anything to that, but went off to find a telephone.

When he was gone, Hilma sat idly turning her cup round and round in its saucer.

Five years' time. Five years of married life with Roger. She would be thirty then. The mould of her married life would have become absolutely set, and she would have become used to the pleasant easy ways of a prosperous existence. She would look back on these days as unreal, very slightly absurd, half forgotten, as she had said.

Or did one perhaps not forget things *quite* so easily?

## CHAPTER SEVEN

As he came back across the room towards her, he smiled, and she thought:

"He's quite unfairly good-looking. No wonder Evelyn decided it wasn't necessary for both of them to have money."

"Well"—he stood looking down at her again from his great height—"you win. Moorhouse is in, and quite willing to see us if we go round there now."

"Come on, then." She stood up with an air of decision. "Let's go at once."

He paid the bill and followed her out into the street, still with that faint air of indecision that made her want to take his arm and say, "Don't be absurd. I've stood up to much more unpleasant things than this."

When they were in the taxi what she did say was:

"Since you now have the unfair advantage of knowing my name, do you think we might even things up by your telling me yours?"

He laughed, and the worried air vanished.

"Yes, of course. It's Buckland Vane."

"Oh." She repeated the name reflectively, and he enquired with more anxiety than the occasion warranted:

"Do you like it?"

"Yes," Hilma said, "I think I do. It's slightly fantastic. Quite in keeping."

"With me, do you mean?" He was not very pleased.

"Um-hm."

"I didn't imagine there was anything fantastic about me."

"Well, perhaps it's more the circumstances in which I met you. Besides, I suppose you're what's called fantastically good-looking," she added calmly.

To her surprise and amusement, he flushed.

"Do you think so?" he said with that odd touch of boyishness.

"Yes. Doesn't Evelyn?" She was smiling teasingly.

"I don't know. I never thought about it." He sounded supremely uninterested in Evelyn's reactions.

"Well, I expect she does." Hilma tried to sound as though it were a very interesting point. Then: "What does one call you for short?"

"Oh, most of my friends call me Buck, of course."

Hilma laughed.

"I told you it was fantastic. Buck Vane! It sounds like someone from the Regency period. The kind of person who gambled madly on a thousandth chance and that sort of thing."

"I'm not the kind of man to gamble on a thousandth chance," he said rather sombrely. "Sometimes I wish I were."

"No? Really? Whatever for?" She was still determinedly gay. "Gamblers nearly always lose."

"Gamblers, Liebling, are not the only people who lose," he said. "Sometimes the steadiest and most common-sense person in the world can lose a great deal."

"I wonder what you mean by that." Hilma smiled casually at him.

But he didn't attempt to tell her, perhaps because the taxi drew up at that moment outside the block of flats.

It gave Hilma a very queer sensation to go once more into that well-remembered building. Even the porter—now on day duty—was the same as on the night of the murder. He failed to recognise her, but, as Hilma glanced at him, she could almost hear him say again, "Terrible business, this murder, isn't it?"

Perhaps she looked a little pale and strained, because, even as they stepped out of the lift at the fourth floor, her companion said:

"There's still plenty of time to go back if you would rather."

"No, of course not." To anyone who could make up her mind as determinedly as Hilma, it seemed quite absurd that a change should be suggested at this last minute. "I don't even want to," she added with perfect truth, for she was more than anxious now to have the whole thing over and done with.

Alan Moorhouse opened the door of his flat himself, and from his slightly truculent air, Hilma felt certain that he had as little liking for this interview as she herself.

That made it much easier somehow, and the perfectly frank smile she gave him as they came into his sitting-room did something towards warming the atmosphere at once.

Probably he did find it a trifle difficult to reconcile the glimpse he had had of her before with the self-possessed girl in the simple but undeniably elegant black-and-white outfit which might have been worn by his own sister.

"Not so much the Piccadilly touch this time," thought Hilma with a good deal of concealed amusement. She supposed no one could look exactly at an advantage upon emerging from behind a curtain at the request of a police officer. No wonder Alan Moorhouse had remembered her in rather lurid terms!

She accepted the chair he offered, but Buck chose to remain standing on the hearthrug, lounging slightly against the side of the mantelpiece. His hands were thrust deep into his pockets, and he was frowning slightly and unhappily. "Looking the picture of guilt, as a matter of fact," thought Hilma.

She smiled up at her host again in that disarming way, and plunged straight into the matter in hand.

"I'm awfully sorry to have caused so much trouble for you and Mr. Vane," she explained earnestly, "particularly as you've neither of you anything to do with me at all and must feel pretty sick at being dragged into my affairs."

"Oh—well——" Alan Moorhouse cleared his

throat. "Very good of you to come along and explain."

"Oh, no, it was the least I could do," Hilma assured him. "You see, it was not Mr. Vane's flat that I meant to come to that night. It was Mr. Martin's."

"*What?*"

She saw she had scored a bull's-eye, so far as surprising her host was concerned.

"Yes." Hilma nodded firmly. "I must explain that I—that I knew Mr. Martin quite well some years ago. It was quite an innocent friendship—though I must ask you to take my word for that. Not that the fact is specially interesting to you, of course," she added. "I was silly enough to write a letter then which he had kept and was going to show my fiancé. It was not at all the kind of letter I should want my fiancé to see—a very difficult letter to explain, however innocent our connection may have been."

"Yes, I see." Almost against his will, her host was interested.

"I expect you read enough about the inquest to gather that he was not above a little profitable blackmail."

"Yes, dirty skunk!" agreed Moorhouse heartily. "I always suspected he was that sort, anyway."

"I was quite—desperate." Hilma bit her lip slightly, because describing the whole thing like this brought back just how desperate she had been. "I decided to go and steal my letter back again. If Mr. Martin had not—had not been killed the evening before, his flat should have been entirely empty on that particular evening. The fact that a light was blazing from the window helped to confuse me. I came up the fire-escape, and let myself into Mr. Vane's flat by mistake."

"Great Scott!" Moorhouse's conversation seemed

by now to have become reduced to half-admiring, half-shocked ejaculations.

"You can imagine how very—embarrassing the whole thing was. For both of us, to tell the truth." Hilma smiled faintly. "But I managed to convince him that I hadn't really intended to burgle his flat."

"The fact that she had already broken open my desk somewhat prejudiced me." The dry interruption was the first part Buck had taken in the conversation.

"Yes, I'm sure Mr. Vane can show you the splintered lock, if you want confirmation," Hilma added eagerly. "No doubt there's still some sort of mark, however well it has been repaired."

"No, no, that's all right." Moorhouse seemed much more interested in hearing the completion of the story than in seeking confirmatory evidence.

"The light in the upstairs flat made us think that Mr. Martin must be there after all, but—but in the hope that he would go out late, as I understand he often did——"

"That's so." Her host seemed quite pleased to be able to confirm some of the evidence on his own account.

"Mr. Vane was good enough to let me wait for a while and he even gave me supper. By then, you understand, he entirely believed my story about the letter."

"Yes. I see." Moorhouse even grinned good-naturedly across at the other man. "Conniving at burglary, eh, Buck?"

"I hope you would have done the same," was the dry retort.

"Oh, absolutely," agreed Moorhouse earnestly.

Hilma smiled faintly.

"But you see how terribly awkward the whole thing

was when the police sergeant came knocking at that unearthly hour."

"Thinking it was some curious scandalmonger like you," Buck informed him amiably, "I thought it best for Miss—Miss——"

"Arnall," supplied Hilma demurely.

"Miss Arnall to hide——"

"Which naturally made me look almost like a self-confessed criminal when the police sergeant discovered me," finished Hilma. "You see, I was actually hiding by the window which gave straight on the fire-escape leading to Mr. Martin's flat. We none of us knew then, of course, that some other poor soul was going to confess to the murder, in any case."

A long whistle from Moorhouse paid tribute to the extreme danger of the position she had been in.

"And so Buck hastily cooked up this story about a disreputable little supper party to give colour to the reason for your hiding?"

"Exactly. It all sounds remarkably feeble now," remarked Buck reflectively. "I can't think why it took in the sergeant for a moment."

"It probably didn't, my boy. I dare say he was as surprised as a policeman ever allows himself to be when someone else deliberately pinned the murder on herself."

"Possibly. But I'm afraid it's been a very nasty experience for Miss Arnall, and of course, you understand we have told you this in the very strictest confidence."

"My dear fellow, *of course!*" Moorhouse's pleasant, somewhat vacuous face looked very grave indeed. "In fact, I'm very sorry, Miss Arnall, to have put you to the unpleasantness of having to come and tell me all this. But—you understand—I thought something quite different. Though, to tell the truth, when you began to speak, I felt pretty sure I'd made a mistake somewhere," he added ingenuously.

Hilma laughed.

"Well, that was rather trusting of you, I'm afraid. Because you didn't really know a thing about me. And of course you were quite right to—to safeguard your cousin's interests."

"Oh, rather. Evelyn's got no father or brothers, you know, or anything like that."

From what she had heard and seen of Evelyn, Hilma felt pretty sure she was capable of looking after herself, but she greeted this admirable sentiment of Alan Moorhouse with a grave nod.

"Then I take it I am cleared of any suspicions against my morals?" Buck observed dryly.

"Oh, of course. I do apologise, old man. But of course, you see how it looked, don't you?"

"Quite. It looked exactly as I intended it to. Only it was meant for the benefit of the police sergeant and not at all for you."

Alan found that very amusing, and insisted on "drinks all round, just to show there was no bad feeling left."

"Well, here's to your marriage, Buck, now we find you're not a Don Juan, after all," he said heartily.

"Thank you." Buck accepted the toast with more politeness than enthusiasm.

For her part, Hilma smiled charmingly and said:

"I hope you'll drink to my marriage too, Mr. Moorhouse. I can assure you I'm glad to feel that this unfortunate business hasn't cast any shadow on that either."

"With the greatest pleasure." Her host bowed very gallantly to her, but, over his shoulder, Hilma observed that Buck put down his glass on the mantelpiece with a very sharp clink.

There was no need to wait any longer now. Hilma glanced at her watch, saw that she would only just have time to get home before Roger came that evening, and said she must go.

"Well, thank you once more for coming." Alan Moorhouse smiled admiringly at her as he held her coat for her.

"Not at all. I'm glad the trouble is cleared up."

They exchanged very cordial good-byes, and then she went out of the flat with her rather silent companion.

"Don't bother to come down. I can find my way myself."

"No, I'd rather take you home."

"You *can't* come all the way home." She frowned a little at him to indicate that he was going too far. But he looked obstinate again.

"Why not? I know your address now. There's no harm in my coming."

"Yes, there is. For one thing, my mother will ask who brought me home by taxi. And for another, I'm late and Roger may already be there. He, too, would wonder who you were."

"Well, can I come part of the way?"

Hilma bit her lip.

"That's what I meant by your 'little boy' manner," she said irrelevantly.

"Oh, lord!" He smiled at that. "I'm sorry. How absurd. But do let me see you safely on your way."

They had reached the street by now, and as a taxi drew up in answer to his signal, Hilma was spared the necessity of further argument.

"Stop near the Albert Hall," he told the driver, and then got into the taxi after her.

"Well," Hilma smiled composedly at him as he dropped into the seat beside her, "now the brilliant marriage is secure again."

"Yes, I have to thank you, Liebling." His tone was perfectly grave.

She shrugged and laughed.

"I should expect you to do the same for me if the positions had been reversed."

"Of course. You know I should be glad to, don't you?"

"It isn't likely to be necessary," Hilma assured him. "Surely even we can't involve ourselves in any more tangles. But"—she spoke rather gently then—"I haven't forgotten that you were prepared to go and fetch the letter for me."

"Oh, *that*!" he dismissed it impatiently.

"Yes, that," Hilma smiled. "It's not such a small thing, you know. If you'd been caught forcing your way into a neighbour's flat, that would hardly have had a good effect on your marriage, I should think."

"No, I suppose not." He smiled. "But one must take a few risks sometimes."

"There wasn't any specially good reason for taking that one," she pointed out. But he didn't answer that. Only his smile deepened in a way she found disturbingly attractive. Perhaps it was that which made her add rather hastily: "Anyway, it's all right now, and we can both—both go our own ways without worrying any more."

"So you won't worry any more—about anything?"

"No, of course not. Will you?"

"No."

They drove in silence for a few minutes. Then he said:

"We're almost there. Thank you, Liebling, for making my marriage to Evelyn quite certain. It was good of you."

"Not at all." She gave him her hand. "Thank you for offering to do the same by my marriage to Roger, if necessary. I shall remember that."

He lightly kissed the hand she had given him, and remarked:

"We have an almost touching concern for the material welfare of each other, haven't we?"

"Of course. We have a rather sharp appreciation of what that means, you see."

He laughed. And just then the taxi stopped, and the driver opened the door with a cheerful, "Here y'are, sir."

It was not possible to make any more of their goodbye after that. (And a very good thing, too, thought Hilma.) They parted as gaily and casually as though they might meet the next night at the theatre. And a moment later the taxi was driving on and Hilma was alone.

She left the taxi a few minutes before she reached home, just in case there might be enquiries about such apparent unwonted extravagance, and when she turned into her road, she saw that Roger's car was already outside.

That was a pity. Roger didn't like being kept waiting, punctuality being one of the minor virtues in which he himself excelled. Well, it couldn't be helped. She would have to say all sorts of silly things about having been shopping and having forgotten the time, and he would want to know where she had been and what she had bought.

For a moment she toyed with the delicious idea of allowing herself to say: "No, I wasn't really doing any of those things. I've been busy establishing an alibi for Evelyn Moorhouse's fiancé."

But, of course, she could never really do anything like that. She thought how amused Buck would have been at her even daring to think of it. Then with a little sigh, she went into the house.

Roger *was* waiting. And, it was quite true, he was not specially pleased about it.

"I'm so sorry, Roger dear." Hilma gave him a quick remorseful kiss, which melted him slightly. "I forgot you were coming early this evening."

"Have you also forgotten that we are going to dinner with the Eltons?" he enquired with slight but unmistakable signs of dipleasure.

She had. And it was difficult for her to hide the fact.

"I won't be a moment changing," she assured him eagerly, and felt irritated that he considered it necessary to take out his watch and look at it. There was a perfectly good clock on the mantelpiece which he might just as well have consulted. But Roger was one of those men who prefer their own time to anybody else's.

Hilma ran upstairs, wondering as she did whether little things like that grew more, or less, irritating as one went on. Perhaps one got used to them. In fact, of course one did. Everyone had one or two tiresome tricks. They just faded into the general background—particularly when there were a number of solid virtues to set against them.

She dressed quickly, in the black dress which she always now called her "burglar dress" to herself, and as she took the velvet cloak and hood from her wardrobe she smiled dryly to think what Roger would have said if he could ever have known how useful this had once proved.

"Poor Roger! My complete burgling outfit," thought Hilma, and even added her scarab bracelet, which she had worn that night with a vague, half-superstitious feeling that it might bring her luck.

"Did it bring luck?" she wondered as she hastily clasped it round her wrist. It was hard to say whether that evening had been lucky or unlucky, all things considered. Anyway, she wore the bracelet this evening more to please Roger than for any other reason. He had given it to her and liked to see her wear it.

Sometimes quite a small thing like that would put Roger in a pleased and satisfied mood for the whole evening.

When she came downstairs again he was talking to her mother, and looked up with an approving smile as she came in.

"My dear Hilma, you certainly have been quick," he said, and even took out his watch again to verify the fact. He himself always took exactly the same time about everything he did, and it seemed to him a real feat that anyone could contrive to change in half the usual time. "You're looking charming, too," he added, and Hilma knew that she was entirely forgiven.

"Yes, charming, dear," echoed her mother. "I hope you have a lovely time."

Hilma smiled and kissed her mother, wondering a little whether the expression "a lovely time" was at all likely to cover an evening spent with a couple of Roger's friends and contemporaries.

However, she was agreeably surprised by the Eltons.

The "first-class cricketer" of Roger's college days had developed into a genial and successful man who had by no means forgotten that, like many other people, he had started as something smaller than he now was. He still had the most refreshing enjoyment of his own success, and was more than willing to help anyone else. His wife and he were evidently devoted, and thought the world of their two very pretty children.

"They're asleep now, of course," Mrs. Elton told Hilma, "but you can come and see them if you like."

So Hilma accompanied her into the firelit night nursery, where two little boys slept contentedly, surrounded by every sign of care and comfort.

"They're sweet," Hilma said with sincerity.

"Yes. I think they're rather nice," agreed her hostess, with extremely ill-concealed pride in them.

Hilma smiled, and thought she was rather "sweet" too. A pretty woman in the middle thirties, Mrs Elton was the personification of kindly, comfortable, gracious living. It was soothing just to stand there with her in the firelit room and look round on all the pleasant but unostentatious things that made up the sum total of her existence.

"I suppose this is more or less how life will be for me," thought Hilma, and the thought brought an indescribably peaceful sensation.

"It must be lovely to have two such nice little boys and a beautiful home," she said half to herself.

"Oh, yes, I'm very lucky," Mrs. Elton agreed with a smile. "But I do know it. I think that's the secret of enjoying things as they come along. Not to take things for granted, I mean."

"Perhaps so." Hilma returned her smile thoughtfully.

"I really get a tremendous amount of pleasure out of the children, for instance. And I always think how fortunate I am that Toby began to be successful fairly early in life. I can have more or less whatever I like for the boys, and none of the anxiety of wondering how it's going to be done. And then, of course, you do get a chance of really enjoying your children when you don't have to do every single thing for them. I don't mean I wouldn't be willing to"— she laughed and patted first one little sleeping head and then the other—"but it's nice to have some of the work taken off your hands so that you're free to enjoy the best of them without being cross and worn out."

"Yes, I know what you mean."

Hilma thought how odd it was that her hostess should have happened to say just these words at just this time.

"Prophetic almost," Hilma told herself. "This nice woman and this charming room might almost typify the life that I've deliberately chosen. It's comforting to know in advance how pleasant it can be."

Turning to Mrs. Elton, she smiled and said:

"Thank you so much for letting me see them. I should have been sorry to miss that."

And she meant it—not only for the interest of seeing the children themselves.

Downstairs they found the men sipping excellent sherry and discussing landscape gardening.

"Yes, that's a splendid idea—splendid idea," Roger was saying. "We might have something of the sort, Hilma." He turned eagerly to Hilma as she came into the room.

She had an odd and pleasant feeling of being admitted into a sort of charmed circle. This talk of children and houses and gardens—all cared for on a lavish scale, without a shred of financial anxiety—was very delightful. It gave one a lovely sensation of being able to stretch mentally and make oneself comfortable.

"You don't mind if we dine rather early, do you?" Mrs. Elton said. "We're taking you on to the theatre afterwards. Toby was able to get tickets for the first night at the Coronet. We thought you would like that."

A pleasant surprise—but all quite by the way—part of the everyday life of these people. It would be part of *her* everyday life, too, Hilma reminded herself. And she felt very contented and happy.

Over dinner, Mrs. Elton said:

"I was sorry not to have a chance of meeting you at the masked ball. We only saw Roger for a few minutes, and you were dancing with someone else or——Oh, no. I remember. You had torn your dress, hadn't you? So tiresome! These things are done in a moment, aren't they?"

Hilma agreed that they were and asked how the Eltons had enjoyed the dance.

"Very much. There were some extremely nice people there, weren't there? You never quite know with these charity affairs who will turn up, but we enjoyed it immensely."

On an impulse she found unable to restrain, Hilma said:

"Wasn't it you who introduced Roger to Evelyn Moorhouse?"

"I expect so. Yes, it was. I remember now."

"A very nice girl," remarked Roger, who meant—though he was honestly unaware of the fact—that he appreciated her financial position.

"Ye-es." Mrs. Elton had rather the air of a truthful person who didn't want to be unkind.

Hilma smiled at her.

"Don't you like her, then?"

"Oh, yes. At least, I think I do. Toby likes her better than I do, to be quite frank."

Her husband laughed.

"You expect too much of a gilded lily, my dear," he told her. "I've known Evelyn Moorhouse since she was so high"—he measured a somewhat improbably short distance from the ground—"and there's never been a thing that she hasn't been able to have. You can't expect a girl like that to be anything but a bit spoilt and autocratic."

"Well, I dare say you're right," his wife admitted doubtfully. "But I think Buck Vane is a good deal too nice for her, all the same. And I often wonder if he knows quite what a handful he's taken on."

"Is that the fiancé?" Roger enquired.

"Yes."

"Well, well, I suppose he wouldn't have asked her if he hadn't wanted her." Life really was as simple as all that to Roger.

"There were rather special circumstances," Toby Elton observed reflectively, at the same time as his wife said:

"I think there is always a certain amount of risk when it's the wife who holds most of the money."

"Oh, certainly." Roger looked shocked. "Is that the situation? Very unsuitable, I quite agree."

"What were the—special circumstances?" Hilma managed that with just the right degree of casual interest, and Mrs. Elton immediately wrinkled her forehead in an obliging effort to remember the facts.

"It's all got something to do with Buck not being left enough money to keep up the family house in Shropshire, and Evelyn wanting to buy the place—ancestors and all, if you know what I mean. Now, let me see. Buck's father died quite young, leaving two sons. Isn't that right, Toby?"

"Yes. Buck was the elder. And the old grandfather, who lived to be goodness-knows-what age, and only died some months ago, never liked Buck——"

"Oh, yes, yes, now I remember the rest of it," interrupted his wife eagerly. "Let me tell it. It's quite like a story. The grandfather really was an old pig. I do know that, because my people come from the same part of the country, and no one had a good word for him. He was the sort of man who re-made his will twice a week for the sheer pleasure of making all his relations grovel."

"And Buck didn't grovel?" suggested Hilma, with a slightly unwise air of being able to answer for that.

"Well, no, I don't expect he did. Anyway, he didn't do whatever it was the old man thought he ought to do, and when the will was read, it was found that Buck *had* been left the family house—the eldest son had to have that in any case—but the wretched old creature had somehow contrived to leave every single penny of cash elsewhere."

"I suppose a man is entitled to leave his money where he pleases," observed Roger sententiously. And Hilma thought how different the same words had sounded when Buck himself had used them.

"Ye-es, of course," Mrs. Elton didn't seem entirely sure that she agreed with that. "Anyway, there was nothing for Buck to do but sell the place——"

"He could have let it," Roger said firmly.

"No, I think it needed a good deal of repairing, or something of the sort. He'd have had to put it in order before anyone would take it, and, if rumour is correct, he just hadn't the money to——"

"I should have thought he could have raised a mortgage." Roger stroked his chin thoughtfully.

Even sweet-tempered Mrs. Elton looked faintly exasperated.

"It may have been mortgaged already. I don't know. Anyway, it was advertised for sale—and Evelyn Moorhouse went down to see it. Some people say she fell in love with the house, and some people say she fell in love with Buck."

"Others say Buck fell in love with her," mocked her husband, "and some unkind people even say he fell in love with her money. But there they are, engaged, and she looks quite satisfied and he seems satisfactorily devoted, and they're going to live at the family home, with all the ancestors and portraits complete. I don't really know why Anne thinks it's anything but a good arrangement."

"Well," Anne Elton looked a little put out, "perhaps it *is*, of course. But I always feel that Evelyn was the kind of person to want to buy a lot of ancestors all complete, you know."

"And a handsome husband thrown in?" suggested her own husband with a smile.

"The man sounds something of a fortune-hunter himself," observed Roger. "I should think *she* is the one who ought to think carefully."

Something about that angered Hilma unreasonably, though she knew that Buck himself would have laughed mockingly and deliberately pointed out the truth of that to her.

"Anyway, he lives in Town at the moment, doesn't he? Where does the country house come in?" she said impatiently. Then, realising the astonishment with which Roger was regarding her, she added hastily: "I mean, someone said he was at the ball the other night, and they spoke as though he lived in Town."

"Oh, he does. That's one of the things that make me wonder if he knows quite how much Evelyn will insist on her own way," Anne Elton said. "There's all this talk about a family house in the country and so on, but I notice that while the season is on, it's definitely Town for both of them."

"Well, well," Roger observed rather heavily. "You know the old saying about paying the piper and calling the tune. I suppose it applies here, too."

"I suppose so," Toby Elton agreed, while Hilma found herself wondering if that were a rule Roger would apply in their own case if there were a dispute. Then she dismissed the idea as most unworthy. And a few minutes later they all rose from the dinner-table and went to get ready for the theatre.

"It's all very well for Toby and Roger to talk," remarked Anne Elton confidentially to Hilma, "but Buck Vane is rather a dear, you know, and I'd hate to think he'd messed up his life with a hasty decision."

"But don't you think," Hilma said slowly, "that he is the kind of man to see things with almost cynical clearness—to weigh them up carefully, and deliberately choose what he thought would be best in the end?"

"Yes—perhaps you're right." Mrs. Elton looked reflective. Then she added in some surprise: "Do you know him then?"

"I—have met him—that's all. That was the impression I had," Hilma said, and then very deliberately spoke of other things.

It was quite a brilliant show at the theatre that night—the kind of evening which would have held Hilma's attention from beginning to end in the ordinary way. But while the people round her laughed and admired, she sat thinking over what she had heard that evening.

So there was really more reason than he had given her for the marriage bargain he had made. She rather admired him for not having gone into more detail about what one might have considered the excuses for his action. That was, of course, if the excuses really existed in the form that Anne Elton suggested.

Hilma remembered very clearly the way Buck had laughed and declared he was an adventurer—that they both were. It was hard to say whether he meant that in all seriousness—in spite of the laughter—or whether he took a slightly harsher view of his behaviour than he need have done.

When they were saying good-night outside the theatre, Mrs. Elton said very cordially:

"I do hope we shall see you again really soon." And Hilma sincerely echoed that. She liked the Eltons immensely, and said as much to Roger on the way home.

"Yes, charming people." Roger voiced his approval with great earnestness. "She's a really womanly woman"—to Roger, praise could go no higher—"and he's a sportsman. Figuratively as well as literally. A wonderful cricketer in his time, you know," he added, under the impression that he had not told Hilma that before.

Hilma smiled and said it had been a delightful evening.

"And I was proud of you," Roger added, though he rather seldom gave vent to such speeches. "You looked splendid, Hilma. Your mother is quite right when she says black suits you."

"It suits all fair people," Hilma told him.

"Yes." Roger looked at her in a very contented way. "And your bracelet and that greeny-blue scarf make a good contrast. Same shade almost, aren't they?"

Hilma laughed, because that was really very observant for Roger.

"That's a nice bracelet." It was one of Roger's less likeable qualities that he always admired his own presents long after he had given them. He even took hold of her wrist to examine the bracelet afresh. And the next moment he gave an exclamation of annoyed dismay: "Why, Hilma, the centre scarab is missing! You must have lost it."

"Let me see!" She was as put out as he was, because she knew, quite apart from the loss itself, that Roger could make a fuss about that sort of thing for weeks afterwards.

It was quite true. A tiny broken ring showed where the scarab had been.

"A splendid specimen, too!" exclaimed Roger. "Dear me, how very unfortunate. It wouldn't have mattered if it had been one of the smaller ones at the side." He sounded just a little as though Hilma should have chosen better when she lost the scarab. "Was it intact when you put the bracelet on?"

"Yes, I—think so." She remembered now how hurriedly she had clasped it round her wrist.

"Surely you would have noticed if it had been missing." There was something like reproof in Roger's tone.

"Yes, I'm almost sure I should." She was not really quite sure, because her dressing had been such a very hasty affair. "I must have dropped it at the Eltons' house—or perhaps even in the theatre."

"Yes, that's possible." Roger was mollified by these suggestions, and even found time to notice Hilma's disappointment and distress. "Never mind, my dear. We'll do our best to find it, and if we don't—well, you must just have another one, that's all." It gave him a good deal of pleasure to be able to say that.

"It's very kind of you, Roger." As his chagrin decreased, hers illogically mounted. She was glad Roger was no longer annoyed about it, and it was characteristically generous of him to offer her another scarab to replace the lost one. But—totally unsuperstitious though she was in the usual way—Hilma had an odd impression that the luck of that evening with Buck was bound up with the bracelet after all.

"I wish I could find it! I wish I could find it!"

Hilma told herself worriedly. "I feel that if I don't, something *else* will go wrong because of that visit to the flat."

An entirely absurd idea, of course, but one that persisted, in spite of all she could do to prevent it.

## CHAPTER EIGHT

ENQUIRY at the theatre during the next few days, and a telephone message of the Eltons' house failed to bring the lost scarab to light, and Hilma resigned herself to the loss with more equanimity than she had felt possible on the first evening.

The idea of ill luck which she had associated with the loss passed in the light of a little common-sense reflection. It was unfortunate—but these things did happen. And, anyway, there were a great many other things to engage her attention just then.

The conversation with Alan Moorhouse and the complete clearing up of all the trouble connected with that ill-starred burgling attempt of hers had lifted more of a weight from her mind than she had realised at first. She really was free now to enjoy the preparations for her wedding and to savour in anticipation the easy, pleasant life ahead, of which she had had such a charming foretaste in her visit to the Eltons.

Her mother joined very happily in shopping expeditions, and Barbara came in more than once to offer advice—wanted or unwanted—on what would suit her cousin and what would not.

"Though, as a matter of fact, Hilma," she declared generously, "there are very few things that *don't* suit people of your colouring. You'll make a marvellous bride, my dear—and Roger will make a good figure, too, so long as playing a star rôle doesn't make him feel a fool."

"Really, Barbara!" The protest came from Mrs. Arnall. "I don't know why it should."

"No, nor do I," agreed Barbara imperturbably. "But the fact remains that he does get all self-conscious if he thinks anyone is looking at him. You'd better tell him, Hilma, that no one bothers about the bridegroom. Except the bride—sometimes," she added carelessly.

Hilma laughed.

"Well, he has plenty of time to get up his courage. It isn't for seven or eight weeks yet."

"Um-hm. Pity he isn't *dark*, now I come to think of it," Barbara said reflectively. "With you so fair, a big dark man would make a wonderful foil. Still, I don't expect even that consideration would make Roger dye his hair. Would it, Roger?" she demanded as he came in just then.

Roger had not heard the rather shattering suggestion, and it had to be repeated.

"Don't be absurd, Barbara. I couldn't possibly think of such a thing," he assured her annoyedly.

"No, I was afraid not," Barbara agreed.

Roger looked at her with something like distrust. Not that he disliked Hilma's lively cousin, but, really, sometimes the girl's idea of a joke became rather personal. Besides, she and her husband were always arranging to do things in a hurry. Roger liked to give thought and consideration to most things he did, and the Curtises' easy habit of rushing hither and thither, usually accompanied by several other people, always made him slightly nervous and put out.

Even that evening they had some wild scheme (as

Roger phrased it) on hand. Jim had joined the party later in the evening, and now they wanted to go on somewhere else, taking Hilma and Roger with them.

"It's quite an informal, after-theatre sort of party," Barbara explained. "The Burnthorpes—they wanted us to go to the theatre with them, but we couldn't, as we were coming here. Then they asked us to join them *after* the theatre and bring you along."

"Surely it's a little late," began Roger. While Hilma said:

"Wasn't that where you wanted us to go before? They seem to hold a lot of informal parties, Barbara."

"Oh, they do." It was Jim who answered. "Awfully jolly people. There's always a crowd there." He evidently felt he could hold out no greater inducement for going there.

"Well, you go along." Hilma smiled. "I don't imagine they really expect us, too."

"But they *do*, Hilma. I've told them quite a lot about you. They'll think it funny if you refuse a second time."

Hilma could not help thinking that people who gave such frequent and casual invitations to strangers probably hardly noticed whether they were accepted or not. But as both Barbara and Jim insisted on the possibility of the Burnthorpes being hurt, she agreed to go with Roger.

"Will you be very late, dear?" Mrs. Arnall enquired, as Hilma stayed behind to kiss her good-night while the others went out to the car.

"I don't expect so" Hilma smiled and shook her head. "I imagine we shall say 'Hello' to a lot of people we've never seen before and are not likely to see again, have a couple of drinks and come away again. There isn't likely to be anyone I know there."

But in this Hilma was wrong. The first person she saw when they entered the large and crowded flat of the hospitable Burnthorpes was Buck Vane.

He was standing in one of the deep window embrasures, talking to an elderly man, and his slight but charming air of deference was oddly out of keeping with the noisy, cheerful, casual people round him.

Hilma was surprised to find how well she withstood the shock. She accepted a sort of flying introduction to her host and hostess with perfect calmness, noticing *en passant* that they displayed none of the frantic interest which Barbara had implied.

Both Barbara and Jim seemed to be known to most of the people there, and they evidently felt they could do Hilma and Roger no better service than to introduce them to as many people as possible in as short a time as possible.

None of the introductions really arrested Hilma's attention beyond a smile and a conventional word or two until Barbara's gay, rather high-pitched voice said:

"And this is Evelyn Moorhouse, of course. But you met before, didn't you? Oh, no, it was Roger, not you. Evelyn, this is my cousin Hilma Arnall."

In the time which had elapsed between the masked ball and this evening, Barbara had evidently progressed by characteristically easy stages from the "Miss Moorhouse" style of address to "Evelyn."

Hilma found herself returning the greeting of a slim, dark girl with unusually light grey eyes. It was her eyes that one noticed before anything else. Though brilliant, they had a cool shallowness about them which made their owner seem oddly remote, in spite of her perfectly cordial manner.

So this was Buck's fiancée.

Well, he had been right when he spoke of her outstanding smartness. Not only were her clothes expensive—they were also very well chosen and most beautifully worn. Every hair of her slightly eccentric coiffure was in place, and the little jewellery she wore was in impeccable taste and undeniably excellent.

She and Hilma stood there for a few moments, talking together—of the play, which Hilma had seen on another occasion, of the near approach of Christmas, of their mutual friends, the Eltons.

Then just as they were about to part company once more, Buck coolly joined their group, and Evelyn made casual introductions.

To an outward observer, there was nothing at all remarkable about Buck's expression. But Hilma knew quite well what that sparkle in his dark eyes meant. He was intensely amused, as well as pleased, that they should meet again like this.

It amused Hilma, too—though she supposed it ought, rather, to shock her—and for a moment the rare dimple showed in the centre of her cheek.

Roger made himself agreeable—however much he might be recalling the criticisms he had expressed to the Eltons—and Barbara remarked:

"You four must be getting married about the same time. Your wedding is just after Christmas, too, isn't it, Evelyn?"

Evelyn agreed that it was, and Roger immediately brought up his remark about it being a good opportunity to combine one's honeymoon with an escape from the English winter.

"How funny—we thought the same thing," Evelyn said, a little drawlingly because she didn't like other people to have the same ideas as herself. "But of course it isn't settled yet. There's plenty of time to change one's mind."

"Only about the honeymoon, I hope," said Barbara laughingly. "I see you're not wearing your ring."

"Oh!" Evelyn looked down at her hand with an exclamation. "Isn't it terrible? I'm always doing that. Now where did I leave it this time?"

At that moment their hostess tore herself away from half a dozen other guests to come hurrying over.

"Evelyn, your ring again! You left it on the dressing-table."

"Thanks, darling."

Evelyn accepted the ring quite coolly—not, Hilma thought, as though it mattered very greatly to her. But perhaps that was just her rather studiedly indifferent manner.

It was a very beautiful ring, Hilma noticed, with a curious, antique setting. Not the sort of ring one would see twice. Rather the kind of ring one might expect Buck to choose.

"It's a good thing you're a patient man, Buck." Evelyn smiled at her fiancé. "Some men would get very wild with me for my carelessness."

"That *might* effect an improvement," Roger could not resist pointing out. But Buck laughed and shook his head.

"Nothing improves Evelyn on that point. She leaves things about even when they aren't strictly detachable. I've something here of yours, Evelyn—that reminds me." He felt in his pocket. "Heaven knows how you managed to get rid of this. It must have been fastened to a chain or a bracelet or something."

He held out his hand, palm upwards, and in the centre reposed a very fine blue-green scarab.

"Lucky for you, my dear, that I have a super-careful domestic staff," he declared with a smile. "This was returned to me with due ceremony from the unromantic vitals of the vacuum cleaner. See to what depths you'd reduced the glories of Egypt!"

"But I'm not guilty for once." Evelyn took the scarab and examined it. "It's not mine."

Hilma was absolutely still, her gaze riveted to the little blue-green object which they were all examining with laughing interest.

"Oh, Buck! Who's your other girl-friend?"

"Evelyn, he's got an Egyptian past!"

"It isn't even as though you have a sister, Buck!"

Everyone was laughing and exclaiming. Everyone that was, except Hilma and Roger. She could not possibly bring herself to look at him. She could only hope that his horror of drawing attention to himself would override his tendency to say exactly what was in his mind. If only he wouldn't exclaim, "Why, Hilma, it's yours!" That would give her time to think of something—something to say when the inevitable questions came.

Roger didn't say anything. It was Buck who spoke —calmly and with a certain amount of amusement in the face of all the mock accusations.

"I may not have a sister, but fortunately have a few tame girl cousins. I refuse to have my reputation wrecked on the jewellery of one of them."

"Well, that *sounds* all right." Evelyn gave a cool little laugh as she handed back the scarab to Buck. "Lucky for you I'm not a suspicious person."

"Very lucky, my dear," Buck said, and smiled at her so nicely that it would have disarmed most people, and quite obviously restored Evelyn's slightly ruffled good humour.

From his expression, Hilma felt almost certain that he *did* imagine the wretched thing belonged to a cousin—or derived from some equally innocent source. He had no special reason to connect it with her own unconventional visit—especially as that had taken place so long ago. The scarab must have lain hidden in a corner of the carpet for a long time, and probably quite a number of possible owners had come and gone in his flat since then.

No, the only really agitated members of the group were herself and Roger—and of the two, it was doubtful which felt more worried and put out.

If only she could think of some adequate explanation! As it was, her mind felt dull and solid. And soon they would have to be going, and certainly nothing would keep Roger from expressing his disturbed curiosity, once they were alone in the car.

It was very hard to give any appearance of enjoying oneself in a careless, light-hearted manner, and as for Roger—he had evidently given up even the pretence of doing so.

If only she could have spoken a word or two to Buck—conveyed to him the seriousness of the situation—they might have hit on something that would cover the facts. But it was utterly impossible in these crowded rooms to have anything resembling a private conversation—even without the consideration that Roger would have been astounded to see them doing such a thing.

The party was beginning to break up now. Already good-byes were being said, and the rooms looked less crowded.

"I suppose it's time we were going." Barbara was at her elbow. "Poor old Roger is looking a bit glum, so no doubt he thinks he's frivolled long enough."

"Perhaps so." Hilma even wished at that moment that she could think of some excuse for prolonging their stay—anything that would put off the hour of explanations. But Barbara had already gone to "collect the men," as she put it.

If only they had come in Jim's car! Then she and Roger would not be left alone together. But they had used Roger's car. They were bound to drop Jim and Barbara first at their flat, and from there it was more than a short drive home.

Hilma felt scared by the terrible aloneness of her predicament. She had no one at all she could consult or from whom she could expect help. She remembered how Buck had laughingly declared he would willingly extricate her from any difficult position in exchange for the help she had given him. But she had not even the opportunity of asking his help now.

"Ready, Hilma?" The very graveness of Roger's tones emphasised the urgency for some solution of the problem.

There was none. And, silently, Hilma went out with him to the car.

Barbara and Jim were already installed, still as imperturbably fresh and cheerful as when they had started out.

"There, Hilma! Aren't you glad you came? Aren't they nice people?" demanded Barbara.

"Very nice indeed," agreed Hilma, without going into the question of whether or not she was glad she had come.

"Amazing the number of people they manage to get into that flat without its being too crowded," remarked Jim admiringly. "Method, that's what it is."

"I thought it was crowded—disagreeably so. And very noisy," cut in Roger with such unwonted curtness that they all stared at him.

"Oh, dear," thought Hilma. "He *must* be put out

for him to have contrived to be almost rude. I've never known him do such a thing before."

Certainly he recovered himself enough to converse fairly amiably for the short time left before Barbara and her husband were deposited at their home. But the moment the car drove on again, Roger turned agitatedly to Hilma.

"Now, Hilma! For heaven's sake, what is all this about?"

"All what?" Hilma knew that surprise was futile, but she could think of no other form of prevarication at the moment.

"You *know* what I mean. What in God's name was your lost scarab doing in Mr. Vane's flat?" Poor Roger practically never brought direct mention of the Deity into his conversation. That he did so at this moment was a measure of his agitation.

"And why are you so certain, Roger," asked Hilma with a touch of cool reproof, "that this particular scarab *was* mine?"

Her air of having detected him in a most unworthy suspicion was so good that for a moment it almost passed muster. But Roger had been revolving the other idea in his mind a little too long for him to abandon it lightly. After a moment of shocked pause, he broke out more emphatically than ever:

"Don't be foolish, my dear! You know it was yours. We can't suppose that half London has been losing scarabs and the other half finding them." Roger felt a little picturesque exaggeration was excusable. "Besides, I recognised it. I know something about these things. Though it was not in my hands, I couldn't possibly be mistaken. It's a wonderfully fine specimen. You don't often see such a good one."

There was another slight pause. Then Hilma said with that air of quiet consciousness of innocence:

"Of what are you accusing me, Roger?"

This rather took the wind out of Roger's sails, and suddenly made Hilma feel mean.

"I'm not *accusing* you of anything," he protested. "I'm only asking you to explain a most extraordinary fact."

"And suppose, Roger, that I don't choose to explain?"

"Don't—choose——"

"Suppose the explanation would involve the very private affairs of someone else?" Hilma said gravely, aware that she was simply inventing wildly as she went along.

"But, Hilma, that's ridiculous!" exclaimed Roger with good reason. "The evidence is that you must have been in the—in the bachelor apartment of some man whom I understood you didn't know until this evening. You accepted the introduction to each other as though you were strangers. And yet apparently you've been visiting him in his own flat."

"I have *not*— if by that you mean that I have done it more than once." Hilma was very glad to be able to deny something with the emphasis born of real truth. "I won't deny that I visited him there once—with very good reason——"

"Good reason," muttered poor Roger, who honestly believed that what he called "nice girls" never did such things.

"With very good reason," repeated Hilma. "That reason is not my own private concern, Roger, and —I'm sorry—I can't tell you what it was."

"But I never heard of anything so silly!" Roger's dismay was genuine, if a trifle ludicrous. "I absolutely insist on knowing. Any man would want to know what his fiancée had been doing, in like circumstances."

Again there was a short silence. Then Hilma shrugged slightly and said:

"Then there's only one thing I can do, and I don't think you'll like it."

"Eh?" Roger looked startled.

"I must refer you to Mr. Vane himself."

Roger was evidently a good deal taken aback, though not—to tell the truth—so much so as Hilma herself when she realised just how far she had taken things.

"Look here, Hilma, surely you can——"

"No." Hilma was absolutely firm. At least this would give her a few hours' reprieve. "I don't think, Roger, that you would entirely believe anything I told you at the moment——"

He made a movement of protest to interrupt her, but she went on:

"I don't blame you. It *is* all a bit fantastic and melodramatic. I would much rather you heard the explanation from Mr. Vane—if he chooses to give it. Please, let's leave the subject for the moment. I'm awfully tired and—and a little upset."

Roger, divided between contrition and doubt, hardly knew what to reply, and perhaps it was fortunate for him as well as Hilma that, at this moment, the car turned into the road where she lived.

"You really mean that—that you want me to go and see Vane about this?" Roger looked uncomfortable.

"Yes, please, Roger."

He didn't like it, she saw. But she had left him very little choice.

"All right." He spoke more grimly than she would have thought possible. "I'll go and see him at his place to-morrow. The sooner this is cleared up, the better."

"I think so, too," Hilma said gently. And on this most unsatisfactory note, they parted.

As soon as she got into the house, Hilma ran quietly upstairs. If her mother were asleep she was anxious not to wake her. If she were awake, she must get any discussion over before she took any action about Buck.

Undressing quickly and quietly, she strained her ears all the time for any sounds of stirring from her mother's room. There was nothing. And, as soon as she was ready, she ventured silently downstairs again—to shut herself securely in the sitting-room, where the telephone was.

She was shivering—but with nervous excitement rather than cold—and she found some difficulty in turning the pages of the telephone directory quickly.

She hoped to heaven his telephone number was under his name, and not under the name of the flats. In the agitation of the moment she could not recall what the block was called, and if he simply had an extension from that——

No! Here it was! Buckland Vane. There could not be two of them. Besides, now she saw the address, she recognised it—wondered how she could ever have forgotten it.

She picked up the receiver, dialled the number and waited. It seemed to her ages. She could hear the purr-purr of the call at the other end, and surely, surely, if he were home, he would have answered it by now.

Perhaps he had not gone home yet. Perhaps she ought to have waited longer. She glanced at the clock. It was nearly two now. She *couldn't* wait. She *couldn't* risk coming downstairs again. Oh, why didn't——

The receiver at the other end was lifted, and a well-known voice enquired with a sort of casual annoyance:

"Who the deuce it that at this time of night?"

"Oh, Buck, it's I——"

"*Liebling!*" And then, much more softly—"Liebling, is that really you?"

"Yes. Listen, I've got to talk to you about something."

"All right, don't sound so scared." Again he spoke rather gently.

"But I am scared," Hilma said, though actually she felt her taut nerves relax a little at his voice. "It's about that scarab."

"The what, my dear?"

"The scarab. The one you tried to return to Evelyn to-night. It was mine—I must have dropped it that—that night. Roger recognised it, and now is going to raise heaven and earth to know what I was doing in your flat."

There was a sharp exclamation from the other end of the wire.

"What did you say?"

"Nothing. At least—nothing fit for your ears." Even now there was that undercurrent of amusement in his voice. "What did you tell him?"

"Quite a ridiculous story, really. You understand, I simply had to invent the best thing I could on the spur of the moment."

"Yes. What did you say?"

"I had to admit that I had been in your flat once, but on purely private business—*your* business."

"What business?" he enquired at once in an amused, intrigued tone.

"Oh, Buck, it isn't *funny*. I didn't say what business. I said it was entirely your concern and I couldn't explain without betraying someone's confidence

—yours or someone else's. I was a bit vague about that."

"But surely he didn't swallow that?"

"No, of course not. He said it was too ridiculous for words——"

"Which it was," came regretfully from his end. "Poor little Liebling. Though, I don't know what else you could have said."

"I had to play for time somehow, you see. Anyway, I've told him that it rests with you whether you feel inclined to explain or not. I adopted a lofty and rather feeble silence, which slightly impressed him, but didn't by any means satisfy him. And—oh, Buck—he's going to come and see you to-morrow, to hear what explanation you've got. We *must* think of something."

There was silence, and she asked anxiously:

"Are you still there?"

"Yes, of course. I was only wondering what I could think up in the way of an indiscreet young sister whose reputation was being protected by us both."

"No, that isn't any good," Hilma assured him hastily. "You said in front of him that you had no sisters. Or someone else did."

"Hell, so they did. No, that won't do. We'll have to think of something else."

"Buck."

"Yes, dear?"

"I'm so dreadfully sorry to involve you in this. I wouldn't have, only it seemed the only possible way, and you said—you said——"

"What did I say, Liebling?"

"That as I had saved your marriage with Evelyn, you would always help me, if I needed it, where my own marriage was concerned."

"Of course. Besides, who else should get you out of this, if not I? It's my fault that you were involved in it. If I hadn't been such a fool as to return that thing in public——"

"Oh, well. We might just as well go back to my breaking into your flat. That was the starting point."

She heard him laugh slightly, a little as though he liked to remember that most regrettable beginning of all the trouble.

"Well, it's the end and not the beginning that we have to think of now. This really must be our last fence, Liebling. I'll think of something. Let me see——"

Suddenly, to her horror, Hilma heard quite unmistakable sounds on the upstairs landing. Her mother must have woken up and was coming downstairs.

"Buck, listen! I must ring off. Someone is coming. I don't know what on earth——"

"All right, don't panic. I'll think of something, I promise."

She pulled herself together and spoke quickly and decidedly.

"If you can't think of anything, please tell Roger the exact truth. That lets you out of it, anyway. I've only just realised how badly I've involved you, too."

"Don't worry. We need not do that. I've hours to think up something good. And—Liebling."

"Yes?"

"Sleep well. I'll look after things for you."

The line went dead and, in spite of everything, it was with a smile that Hilma hung up the receiver and turned to meet her mother's astonished gaze.

"Hilma dear, whatever is it? I thought I heard you down here. Are you ill?" Mrs. Arnall trailed over anxiously, clutching a handful of pink negligé as usual.

"No, no, Mother," Hilma spoke reassuringly, "I'm perfectly all right. We got home frightfully late, I'm afraid, and then, when I was just ready for bed I remembered I'd promised some girl at the party that I'd phone her about something."

"At this hour of the morning?" Mrs. Arnall's surprised glance went to the clock.

"Yes. It was an address she wanted urgently. She was leaving very early in the morning, and phoning now saved me from getting up early to answer her call," Hilma explained with a glibness that surprised herself.

"Well, really, I don't know when some of these young friends of Barbara get any sleep at all," Mrs. Arnall declared. But she was satisfied with the explanation, and, as she accompanied Hilma upstairs to bed, she made nothing more than a kindly enquiry as to how she had enjoyed herself.

However, this definitely put an end to any possibility of further telephoning with Buck. It was terrible—but she must leave the whole thing entirely in his hands.

If his marriage had trembled on the edge of disaster over the affair with Alan Moorhouse, hers was in at least as much danger now, and only Buck's resource and invention could save it.

She felt now that she had not told him half enough—that there were a thousand points at which he might give himself away, even if he could think of a convincing story, which was not by any means certain. It was a terrible feeling, to have to leave all your hopes and ambitions in the care of someone else.

But if she had to do that, perhaps there was no one so well qualified to care for them as the smiling, half-cynical man who declared that their motives were so alike, and that their mutual sympathy was based on the fact that they were both something of adventurers.

What was it he had said? Very charming adventurers, of course, but—with that regretful smile of his—adventurers.

But he had also said: "Sleep well. I'll look after things for you."

And on that thought Hilma closed her eyes and fell asleep.

## CHAPTER NINE

HILMA woke slowly and reluctantly the next morning—with that slightly cold, shrinking feeling which is one's instinctive effort to escape from a half-remembered disaster.

As she rose to complete consciousness again, she glanced quickly at the clock.

Her first thought was: "What time would Roger go to see Buck?" Her next: "How had Buck employed the intervening hours? Had he really managed to work up a good story to cover the wretched facts?"

It was no good worrying. She tried to convince herself that the whole thing was out of her hands now, and she could only wait. But it was anything but easy to present a smiling, unruffled appearance to her mother and father. And when Mrs. Arnall happened to mention something about her wedding dress, Hilma felt it was singularly inappropriate to the moment.

"Oh, I don't know, Mother. We'll see about that later," she said hastily in answer to some enquiry.

"Well, we haven't *all* the time in the world left, you

know, dear," her mother assured her complacently. While Hilma thought grimly:

"Perhaps there won't be any need for a wedding dress at all."

Then she wondered why on earth she had not made an attempt to get in touch with Buck early in the morning. She could surely have made some sort of excuse to go out and telephone from a call-box. Now it was too late. If she telephoned, Roger might already be there. On the other hand, he might delay going until the afternoon and she would be in this miserable state of indecision all day.

When her mother suggested that they should go out shopping all the morning, she accepted at first with alacrity, thankful for something to take her thoughts off things. Then, as soon as they were outside in the street, she wondered if Buck might telephone on some urgent point and be appalled to find her away from home.

However, she was committed to the shopping now, and for what seemed like hours she accompanied her mother in and out of shops, earnestly discussing a trousseau which might never be needed.

"We might just as well stay out to lunch, dear." Mrs. Arnall was really enjoying herself. "I don't see any sense in going back to cold meat."

Hilma would far rather have gone home and made some attempt to find out what had happened, but, apart from being unable to find an excuse for doing so, she had not the heart to interrupt her mother's intense and almost childlike pleasure in their day together.

Besides, what did it matter? Hilma had now reached a state of fatalistic certainty that everything had gone wrong. What on earth *could* Buck think of to cover the facts? The only important thing was to make sure that he was not himself involved in the ruins.

With this certainty that her engagement to Roger was as good as broken, it seemed almost sinful to allow her mother to spend a happy afternoon inspecting and discussing the display of very exclusive household linen in a big West End store.

"Not, of course, that there won't probably be nearly everything you want already in Roger's house," she observed with great satisfaction to Hilma. "But you're sure to want to make some additions. And I know from the way Roger has spoken to me that he means to be very indulgent about anything new you want in the house."

"Yes, he's awfully kind over anything like that," agreed Hilma, in what she feared was a rather flat tone.

She succeeded in luring her mother away from the linen department at last, and had just reached the stage of watching her linger lovingly over sundry side-attractions on the way out, when a voice spoke behind her:

"Why, hello, Miss Arnall! It is Miss Arnall, isn't it?" And, turning sharply, she found herself face to face with Buck. A Buck whose dancing eyes and very roguish smile had no suggestion of failure about them.

"Why, Bu—Mr. Vane! Mother, I don't think you've met Mr. Vane, have you?"

The introduction was effected, and Mrs. Arnall made pleasant conversation, while Hilma tried to read from Buck's expression just how things had gone. But she could read nothing there except a charming attention and concern for what her mother was saying.

"I expect you know my daughter is getting married very soon," Mrs. Arnall was saying. "Such a lot of shopping—but women always enjoy that, don't they?"

"So I understand from my fiancée." He smiled down at Hilma's mother with exactly the same interest he would have shown to someone half her age.

"Oh, you're getting married, too? Oh, well then, you know all about it."

"Not really. I suppose a mere male stands outside the final thrills of shopping," Buck declared. "But I receive detailed reports from time to time."

"Mr. Vane is marrying Evelyn Moorhouse, you know," Hilma explained. "You've heard Barbara speak of her."

"Of course. Oh—excuse me just one moment." Mrs. Arnall turned away to hear the report of a shop assistant who had been making some enquiry for her.

"Well?" Hilma spoke softly but urgently.

"All right, Liebling, go ahead with the trousseau."

"You mean the explanation was satisfactory?"

"Absolutely."

"Oh, Buck! How did you do it?"

"Hilma dear, what do you think about this?" Mrs. Arnall, completely unaware of any drama in the low-toned conversation being carried on a few feet away from her, summoned her daughter to a matter of real importance. "Now don't you think the white is just a *little* too hard? That off-white shade is so much more becoming——Yes—would you please hold it up a little more so that my daughter can see how the light falls on it. There, you see what I mean?"

Hilma didn't see at all. She hardly took in what her mother was talking about. She only wanted to get back to Buck and hear what story had been used—what attitude she was to take up when she saw Roger.

"It's lovely, Mother," she agreed enthusiastically.

"The off-white, you mean?"

"Either of them," Hilma said injudiciously.

"Oh, *no*, my dear! There really isn't any comparison, to my way of thinking. You must remember it will be in *daylight*. That always gives a harder effect. Really, Hilma, I do think the off-white——"

"Yes, of course, you're quite right." Hilma hardly knew if it was a wedding-dress or a tablecloth that they were discussing. But, with quite brilliant salesmanship, the assistant blessedly recalled the fact that there was yet another shade to be considered—"a very rich cream, madam"—and while he and Mrs. Arnall discussed that, Hilma escaped again for a moment.

"Buck, what attitude am I to take up?"

"Wear a halo as becomingly as you can. You're a wonderful girl. Saved my young cousin from the blackmailing attentions of our friend upstairs——"

"Buck!" She laughed at the sheer effrontery of that, until she was afraid her mother would notice and wonder what was happening.

"Returned the letters to me in person—having melted his heart. Hence the property left in my flat. Say as little as you can until we've had time to talk things over properly."

"But where? And when? I can't——"

"Ah, *that's* best of all. Hilma dear, *there's* a beautiful shade for you."

With an exemplary show of interest Hilma returned to her mother's side.

"Yes, beautiful, Mother." She really must try to find out for what this was intended. "I think that is the best of the three."

"So do I. If you did decide on satin, you could have

nothing lovelier than that. It would look rich and soft in the daylight *out*side the church, and still not be insipid *in*side."

With a slight shock, Hilma realised that they were discussing the material for her wedding dress.

It was a matter of such exquisite moment that Mrs. Arnall drew even her new acquaintance into the discussion.

"Come and give us the opinion of a mere man, Mr. Vane." She smiled at Buck, who drew nearer at once. "What do you think of that for a wedding dress?"

There was a queer little pause. Then he said with a whimsical little smile:

"Am I really being asked to advise Miss Arnall on the choice of her wedding dress?"

"Well," Mrs. Arnall laughed, "if you're soon going to be a bridegroom yourself, you ought to have *some* ideas on the subject."

"Then I think she would look exquisite," he said slowly. "But have the slightest touch of blue on it somewhere—the same blue as her eyes."

"Why, Mr. Vane, you're quite a dress artist," Mrs. Arnall declared with a smile. "I think that's quite good advice."

Buck bowed to her with a smile in his turn and then it seemed fairly obvious that he could hardly prolong a chance meeting much further. He shook hands with her and left her to the happy problem of the rival satins, contriving, however, to draw Hilma a little way off with him for a few moments.

"Liebling, can you meet me to-morrow?"

"It hardly seems——"

"Yes, it's absolutely necessary. I can't possibly explain here or tell you all the things you're supposed to know. Have you got to see Roger to-night?"

"No. I could have a headache and just phone."

"Good, then do that. And meet me to-morrow afternoon."

"Where? Quick! Mother is going to call me again."

"The same place as before. Just outside the gate. I'll have the car, and we'll drive out a little way. It's safer than any other way."

"All right, three o'clock. No—say half-past two. It gets dark so early now."

"I'll be there. And—Liebling."

"Yes?"

"The cousin you rescued is called Leni."

A smile flickered over Hilma's face.

"Does she really exist?"

"No, of course not."

"But inherits the name from the Austrian part of the family?"

"Correct."

"I think, said Hilma, "you lie with the most superb effrontery I have ever seen in anyone."

"Of course," he agreed. "The adventurer to the life." And, raising his hat with a brilliant smile, he turned away and left her.

Hilma went back to make the final decision about her wedding dress. It seemed to her to take more time and thought than the matter warranted. But perhaps that was because she was already a little tired of her day's shopping.

Afterwards, when they were going home, her mother said to her, "What an extraordinarily charming man, Hilma. So he's marrying the Moorhouse heiress?"

"Yes. They make a very nice couple," Hilma told her gravely. "Evelyn Moorhouse is good-looking, too, you know."

"And is he as rich as she is?"

"No, I don't think so."

"Well, I suppose one couldn't have everything," Mrs. Arnall admitted reasonably. "When a man's as good-looking and charming as that, it's asking too much of the gods to make him wealthy, too. Besides, she has enough for both, if all they say is true."

"Yes," Hilma agreed. "She has enough for both."

"That was really very penetrating of him about your needing a touch of blue on your wedding dress." Mrs. Arnall looked thoughtful. "Not many men bother to notice details like that—at least, not for absolutely casual acquaintances."

"I suppose not," Hilma agreed. She was glad there was not much need for her to do anything but agree in slightly varying phraseology to her mother's statements. It meant that she was free to think about the meeting to-morrow. Or rather—for she must remember that this came first—of what she was going to say when she spoke to Roger on the telephone.

She had only a fairly meagre supply of information really, and she would have to go carefully in order not to give herself away. One thing was fairly straightforward—she could easily make the long day's shopping a reason for feeling too tired and having too much of a headache to want to see anyone that evening.

"Poor child!" her mother exclaimed sympathetically, when she pleaded the headache. "Really, I believe I stand up to this sort of thing better than you do. But then, of course, it's all rather more worrying for you. I only do the advising. It's you who have to do the final choosing. But really, Hilma dear, I think you've made a *very* wise choice for your wedding dress."

Hilma smiled and agreed, while she secretly wondered rather guiltily if all girls grew as sick of the sound of their wedding dresses as she was at that moment of hers.

"I think I'll ring Roger, just in case he was thinking of coming round to-night," she said. "I'd rather not have anyone here this evening."

"I should, dear. He'll quite understand, after the late night you had yesterday. Better go to bed early," her mother declared, and tactfully went out of the room while Hilma put through her call to Roger.

As Hilma sat there, idly waiting for her call to come through, she tried to recapture some of the anxiety which she had felt last night at the idea of her marriage plans going awry. If she could have been so agitated about that, then it must mean that she valued her marriage very highly.

Well, she did, of course. She only had to recall the kind of life she had seen mirrored in the Eltons' home, to realise how much all this planning and safeguarding meant to her. She wondered if Buck thought about his country home in the way she pictured *her* kind of life. She supposed he must. After all, if he was prepared——

"Hilma, my dear! Is that you?" From Roger's tone she realised at once that he was prepared almost to abase himself for the unjust suspicions he had entertained against her. It made her profoundly uncomfortable—not only because she didn't like Roger doing that sort of thing, anyway, but also because she felt she was remarkably little deserving of the opinon he now had of her.

"Yes. I just rang up to ask if you——"

"Yes, my dear, indeed I did. And I can't tell you how sorry I am for anything I implied last night. Really, Hilma, I'm afraid it was late and I was tired and quite ridiculously suspicious——"

"No, it wasn't ridiculous of you," Hilma told him

firmly. "I don't know what else you could have thought, Roger. *Please* don't blame yourself."

"Oh, but I do—I most certainly do." She had a faint suspicion that Roger was almost enjoying blaming himself. He felt it was so right. "Of course, Vane explained the whole thing to me—said he couldn't possibly have you under a cloud because of your generosity. But, my dear, I'm really horrified when I think of your approaching that scoundrel by yourself."

For a moment she thought he meant Buck. Then she realised that the conversation had passed over to references to Charles Martin.

"Oh, well, there didn't seem anything else to do." She hoped that was right.

"Extraordinarily brave of you, Hilma. Poor misguided girl!"

This must be the non-existent Leni, and not herself, she supposed, and suddenly, with an enjoyment which she felt only Buck would have appreciated, she added a few artistic details:

"Well, she was very young, Roger, and a nice kid, really. It would have been awful to let her mess up her whole life for lack of a little courage."

She had a funny feeling, as she said that, that she was speaking, not of the fictitious Leni, but of the impulsive, incautious girl that she herself had been at twenty.

"Very generous of you, my dear, and most understanding." Roger sounded slightly sententious, as he always did when he used such expressions.

"Oh, no. Anyway, it's all over and done with now. Of course, you'll never say a word about it, will you?"

"My dear Hilma! As though I should!" This, she felt, was perfectly sincere. Roger had a horror of concerning himself with other people's affairs, and was the last man on earth to let slip some indiscreet remark about any confidence that had been made to him.

She gave a little sigh of thankfulness, and, as she pushed back her hair with her disengaged hand, she realised that she genuinely had a headache after all this strain and worry.

"Roger, I don't know if you meant to come round to-night——"

"Indeed I did. I feel I owe you my apologies in person." Even over the telephone Roger's voice sounded grave and weighty. She felt glad that she had an excuse for escaping from yet more apologies.

"Well, please don't bother, dear."

"Hilma, it's no *bother*. I hope I know when I am in the wrong."

Hilma wished impatiently that he didn't know it in quite so much detail. But her voice was perfectly calm and quiet as she said:

"No, dear, I didn't mean it that way. I don't want you to blame yourself any more, as a matter of fact. But what I really wanted to say was that I'm very tired and have a headache. Make it to-morrow instead of to-night. I'd much rather go to bed early to-night."

"Well, of course—if that's how you feel." Roger was a little reluctant really to give up his state apology.

"I do," Hilma insisted firmly.

"Then of course we'll do as you say. To-morrow afternoon, then? We could——"

"No, evening, Roger."

"I thought we might drive out into the country if it's as fine as to-day."

Hilma wanted to scream, but managed to control herself.

"I'm awfully sorry, I can't manage the afternoon, Roger. But I'll be home by six, anyway."

"Very well. And you really feel quite all right about—about this little trouble?" It was not within Roger's capacity to ask if he were forgiven. That was much too emotional a word.

"Quite all right," Hilma assured him. "Only promise me not to worry about it any more."

With a certain amount of pleasurable reluctance, Roger promised not to worry any more, and Hilma was at last free to ring off and indulge in a perfectly genuine headache.

As she passed through the hall on her way upstairs, her mother came out from another room and said:

"Well, what did he say?"

"Oh, he apolo——" Hilma stopped suddenly, remembering that her mother knew nothing whatever about this business. "About what, Mother?" She looked a little vague.

"Why about the material for the wedding dress, of course, child! Whatever else could you have been talking about all this while?"

"Oh!" Hilma smiled. "I didn't tell him about that. Isn't it unlucky or something to discuss your wedding dress with your fiancé?"

"No, of course not, you silly girl. It's unlucky for him to see you in it before your wedding day, but you can *tell* him about it as much as you like."

"I'll tell him to-morrow," Hilma said. "There's plenty of time."

And then she went upstairs.

## CHAPTER TEN

EVEN before she opened her eyes next morning, Hilma knew that it was a beautiful day. This was a very different awakening from that of the previous day.

She sat up in bed, smiling with pleasure to see the bright winter sunshine, smiling to remember that all her troubles were really over at last, and smiling just a little because she was meeting Buck this afternoon.

It would be a sort of salute to success. A mutual acknowledgment that, oddly enough, with the help of each other, they had surmounted all difficulties and were about to attain their respective ambitions. They certainly had reason to congratulate themselves and each other.

It was no surprise to Hilma that everything went smoothly this time. There were no awkward questions at home, no need to invent any explanations for her mother, no interruptions in her plans as she had made them.

This time it was he who had arrived first, and as Hilma came in sight of the gate, she saw a sleek little black Jaguar drawn up at the side of the road.

He got out as she came up to him, and she saw that he, too, was smiling and in good spirits.

"Liebling"—he took her hand a little ceremoniously—"we meet on the crest of the wave to-day, I think."

"We do." She returned his smile. "Thanks to——"

"Each other," he assured her.

"Well, yes, I suppose that's right," Hilma agreed with a laugh.

"Please." He held open the door of the car for her,

and he carefully tucked a fur rug over her before going round to the driving seat himself. "Warm enough?"

"Perfectly, thanks. What a lovely little car."

"Yes. Part of our natural background," he explained.

"Yours, if you like. I haven't anything like this."

"But you will have, Liebling."

"No," Hilma said. "No, I can't imagine Roger allowing me to race around in a little car all my own. But of course I shall be able to use the Rolls more or less when I like."

"One can always make do with a Rolls," Buck assured her, and they both laughed.

"Now tell me all about it," Hilma said.

"About yesterday?"

"Of course."

"Well, Liebling, he arrived in a great state very early. I felt sorry for him. He's a good fellow, you know," he added reflectively. "Almost too good a fellow for a golden-haired adventuress like you."

"Buck, I'm not——"

"We agreed about that long ago," he warned her.

"All right. Go on."

"He was much more gentlemanly than I was about it. Wandered round and round the point until it was all I could do not to show I had been forewarned by leading him straight to the subject. He quite hated himself for entertaining any suspicions about your being anything but a sweet girl. Whereas, of course, he ought to have known by one look at you——"

"Not," Hilma retorted sweetly, "unless he had the same kind of scheming mind and acted from similar unworthy motives."

"Ah, perhaps that is the secret of it," Buck admitted, smiling ahead down the road. "Well, anyway, we got to the point eventually. And then I flatter myself I gave an excellent representation of a noble-hearted fellow who could not allow someone to shoulder blame unfairly."

"That," Hilma said, "must have been rather difficult for you."

"On the contrary, Liebling, the part fitted me like a glove. We adventurers can turn our hand to almost anything, you know."

"I dare say," Hilma agreed, and the dimple appeared in the centre of her cheek.

"I explained to him about Leni. A charming girl—from the Austrian side of the family, as you yourself observed. He quite understood, of course, that the slightly foreign element explained a great deal. No harm in the child—in fact, I grew quite fond of her as I described her wayward disposition—but she had been very indiscreet. I could hardly be too thankful that she had met a steadying influence like yourself."

"Buck! You *didn't* say these ridiculous things!"

"More or less. Why not? They supplied the perfect background to my story. She confided in you, of course—not me—and as you had known Martin in the old days, you boldly went and demanded the foolish letters which my poor little cousin had written. It said very much for your strength of personality, Liebling, that he handed them over. And then—and this was your master-stroke—you brought them to the serious-minded cousin."

"*You?*"

"Certainly me. Destroyed them in front of me, but suggested I should keep a very careful eye on my indiscreet little cousin in future."

"And what," asked Hilma grimly, "was the effect on you?"

"I, Liebling? I was horrified that such a thing could have been going on in the very block of flats where I myself lived. I have sent Leni into the country. I'm sure you'll agree that's the best place for her."

"Oh, unquestionably." Hilma laughed a good deal. "But did my poor Roger really swallow all this whole?"

"Yes. But of course, it sounded much quieter and more circumstantial when I served it up to him," admitted Buck modestly. "I merely suggested the outlines, and left discreet imagination to fill in the rest."

"It seems a shame, doesn't it?" Hilma bit her lip.

"That I should have to tell so many lies for you?"

"No. That poor Roger should be made to listen to them."

"Well, Liebling, if we'd told him the exact truth, what would have happened?"

"Yes, I know. It doesn't make one feel any better, though. I sometimes find it difficult to remember that all this came of writing one silly letter, on a wrong and absurd impulse which I failed to live up to."

He nodded sombrely, and the laughter suddenly went out of his eyes.

"I know. I sometimes ask myself just where one stops being a fool and starts to be a scoundrel."

There was silence then while he drove rather rapidly.

"Buck."

"Um-hm."

"Do you often think on those lines?"

"No, Liebling, very seldom. Most of the time I know exactly what I want, and exactly what I am prepared to do in order to get it."

"And now you're very near attaining your final ambition?"

"Very near."

"It's a—good feeling, isn't it?"

"Do you mean virtuous or enjoyable?"

"You know quite well what I mean."

He laughed then.

"You know the feeling, too, don't you?"

"Yes." Hilma spoke thoughtfully. "Yes, I'm pretty satisfied with things at the moment. Nearly losing everything does make you appreciate it."

"You had a bad fright over that confounded scarab, didn't you?"

"Yes, I did. So did you over Alan Moorhouse, didn't you?"

"Quite right, Liebling. I saw the whole family estate vanishing into thin air because I'd hidden a pretty burglar behind a window curtain."

She glanced quickly at him and saw that he was smiling again, though he pretended to be intent upon his driving.

"I hope," Hilma said gravely, "that you remember it to the pretty burglar's credit that she came and cleared you afterwards."

"Believe me, Liebling, I shall always remember it," he assured her. "Even when I've become a middle-aged and gaitered squire, I shall look over my estate sometimes and think: 'Now this would all belong to a stranger if it had not been for—Liebling.' "

Hilma was quite silent for a moment. Then, when she did speak, her voice was rather gentle.

"It means an awful lot to you, that estate, doesn't it, Buck?"

"Well, my dear, it represents all the life I'm used to." He spoke quite seriously for once. "I don't know if you know much about English country life. It gets hold of you—especially if the generations before you have known it and loved it. It isn't an easy thing to tear your roots out of the soil."

"And so, when you got a chance to leave them there undisturbed—you took it?"

"Exactly."

"Yes, I think I understand. Somebody told me—quite by chance—about the—the way your grandfather left things."

"And added that I was therefore marrying Evelyn purely for her money, I suppose?" he added grimly.

"Well—no, not exactly. She seemed more impressed by the idea that Evelyn was marrying you for your ancestors, so to speak."

"Oh!" He laughed shortly. "It isn't quite as cut and dried as that, you know. As a matter of fact, Evelyn and I get on extremely well together. We're neither of us specially sentimental, we like more or less the same things, and, to put it with absolute brutality, each has something the other wants."

"Yes, I can imagine that. I suppose many happy marriages have been built on less," Hilma said slowly.

"One likes to think so. I think she finds me moderately attractive. I find her the same—perhaps more than that. She hasn't any absurd, endearing little ways or——" He stopped abruptly and then frowned. "I have no right to talk like this. I shouldn't to anyone else, of course."

"No, I know. It's just that, somehow, we have rather stripped things to the bone when we've discussed things together. It seems to come naturally. Perhaps there's no harm in it. I suppose it started with our both being so frank when we never expected to meet each other again."

"Yes, that's it." He smiled suddenly. "Funny how we were both so certain it was the briefest, isolated meeting. And all the time our stories had got tangled up in the most fantastic manner."

Hilma nodded.

"As you said when we met to-day, we really owe it to each other that we've worked out our stories to a satisfactory conclusion. *That's* the queerest part of all."

"But rather nice, don't you think?"

She agreed with a laugh, and then added quickly

"Oh, Buck, do stop here. It's so lovely."

He drew up at once by the side of the road.

They were right out in the open country by now, and on either side of them stretched bare, almost leafless woods. Here and there a brown, withered leaf still clung to a thin branch, flickering restlessly to and fro and looking like a great moth outlined against the pale blue of the winter sky.

Scarlet creeper sprawled over some of the tree-trunks in extravagant abandon, oddly at variance with the prim little stream that chattered past over roots and pebbles, to lose itself under a small stone bridge which spanned the valley.

"Would you like to get out and walk a little?" He smiled slightly at the pleasure in her eyes.

"Yes, do let's."

"You won't be cold?"

"No, of course not." She already had the door of the car open, and a moment later stood at the side of the road, where it sloped down to the little bridge.

He took her hand, and she could feel the support of his strong fingers as he helped her down the stony slope.

"There you are. Now you can look over into the stream."

"It's pretty, isn't it?" Hilma leant her arms on the

moss-covered parapet, and after a moment he did the same.

"Yes, it's pretty. In a terrific hurry, isn't it?"

"Um-hm. Poor little thing, it's impossible to believe it ever does really reach the sea."

"Nonsense, Liebling," he said mockingly. "Nothing should seem impossible to you to-day. Not after all the difficulties we've successfully surmounted."

She smiled.

"Yes, it is rather our great day, isn't it?"

"It is."

"I suppose you have the same feeling that I have—that nothing further can go wrong. I didn't have that feeling at any other stage of our—adventure. I felt uneasily that something would still go wrong, though I couldn't quite say what."

"And all the time it was the scarab," he suggested with a laugh.

"Well, it seems to have been a dozen other things as well. But of course, that was the final disaster."

"But now it's all over?"

For some reason she disliked that way of putting it. She hastily amended it to:

"Now it's all safely and happily over."

"Yes," he agreed lightly. "It all started with mutual distrust over a broken lock, and ends very charmingly with mutual congratulations in a charming winter landscape."

Hilma watched with great attention the progress of a leaf down the stream. Then she said:

"They're very sincere congratulations as far as I'm concerned, you know. I do really hope that you'll be most awfully happy with Evelyn."

"Thank you, Liebling. I hope you'll be very happy with your Roger."

"Oh, I shall be," she said quickly. "I never told

you, but I went to see some friends of his some time ago. Nice, kindly people with lots of money. They live very much the way we shall. I thought how I should like it. They have two lovely children—a beautiful house—marvellous garden."

"In fact, everything you want, Liebling?"

She didn't answer.

"I suppose that will be my lot, too, if I'm lucky. Lovely children—a beautiful house—marvellous garden."

Still she was silent.

They both watched the stream for quite a long time. Then he said very quietly and deliberately:

"My darling, it isn't the slightest good. I simply can't do it after all."

"What—do you mean?" Hilma spoke in a whisper, and suddenly she found she was trembling so much that she was glad to have the little stone parapet to lean on.

"Liebling," he said, "I mean exactly what your silence meant when you wouldn't answer my question just now. I mean that the house isn't the slightest good unless it's our house—the garden isn't the slightest good unless it's our garden—and above all, the children aren't possible unless they are *our* children. I couldn't have another woman's children. That's the beginning and end of it. And I don't believe you could bring yourself to have any man's son but mine."

Even then she didn't look at him. Only she slowly pushed her hand along the stones until it rested on his.

"Buck, I'm not a bit good at making a little money go a long way."

"No. And I'm probably not much good at making money at all until I've had a bit more practice."

"You—hate hard living, don't you?"

"Hate it. So do you, don't you?"

"Yes. I'll be quite honest. I'm—frightened of poverty."

"So am I, Liebling. Only I'm much more frightened of life without you."

"We're not much good as adventurers, after all, are we?"

"Not much, darling."

He put his arm round her and drew her against him. She leant her head against his shoulder and said:

"Buck, what about your family home?"

"I don't know. I suppose I can sell it."

"But you love everything to do with the past of your family, don't you?"

"Um-hm." He very softly put his lips against the side of her cheek. "But there's such a thing as loving the future of one's family, too."

"You mean you'd sell it without breaking your heart about it?"

"I think so. We shouldn't make much out of it, as a matter of fact. It's heavily mortgaged. But I suppose there'd be something."

"Buck, *I* haven't anything at all to contribute—except some unsuitably extravagant things towards a trousseau."

"You have some lovely stuff for a wedding-dress, I think," he said with a smile.

"Oh, yes." She laughed a little. "But even that belongs to Aunt Mary, in a way, I suppose. She paid for my trousseau because she approved so heartily of Roger. She wouldn't approve a bit of you, Buck."

"I can't blame her."

"She'll probably say I owe her the money she advanced because I got it on false pretences or something like that."

"She must be distressingly like my grandfather.

Well, we'll have to sell the car and pay her. You must have your trousseau, even if you're marrying a penniless adventurer."

She moved slightly against him.

"Buck, *is* there any work you can do?" she asked with candour.

"Well, Liebling, I know a good deal about farming and estate management. I suppose I must set about looking for a job as a bailiff."

"Oh, that doesn't sound at all like you."

"My darling, does any of this sound at all like either of us?"

"No. But"—she looked up at him suddenly and smiled full into his face—"it's lovely, isn't it?"

The half-cynical, half-humorous expression vanished suddenly.

"Liebling, it's the most wonderful thing that ever happened to two groping, rather blind people. Do you realise that we've both been fighting against this ever since you shoved a penknife under the lock of my desk?"

She laughed and hid her face against him.

He looked down at her with the utmost tenderness and said softly:

"And do you realise that it was in the very moment Fate had handed our highest ambitions to us on a silver plate that we knew no ambitions mattered beside having each other?"

She didn't answer him, and he bent his head to whisper:

"Why don't you speak to me?"

"I'm listening to your heart."

"Why, you absurd darling?"

"Because you told me once that you hadn't got one."

"Did I, Liebling? Well, I'm not sure that it wasn't true then."

She shook her head, and he looked amused.

"Not true? How do you know?"

"Because," Hilma said, "it's responsible for all the trouble. Here we planned and planned, worked out everything as coolly and sensibly as could be, agreed on the cynical, hollow value of most things, and had almost achieved brilliant marriages. And then your heart must needs get out of control and spoil everything."

"I like that! What happened to yours, I should like to know?"

"Oh, that's different." The dimple appeared in Hilma's cheek. "Whatever happened to *my* heart, I had to keep quiet. It was only you who could speak, and since you couldn't manage your own heart—you did speak."

"And all our gilt-edged plans went up in smoke?"

"Exactly."

"It seems a lot of trouble to be caused all by one man's heart," he said gravely.

"It is."

"Hardly seems worth it, Liebling. Perhaps you'd better break it right away before it does any more damage. You know the way."

"Buck!" She flung her arms round him and, laughing, he caught her and covered her face with kisses.

It was a long while before she said:

"I suppose we ought to go now."

"Well, there are a lot of unpleasant things to settle," he admitted with characteristic candour.

"Wouldn't it be awful if we hadn't got each other?" she said as they made their way back to the car.

"Managing all these ghastly re-arrangements, with everyone disapproving, I mean?"

"Quite unbearable, darling, except that, if we hadn't got each other, we should not be doing this absurd and wonderful thing at all. We should be getting comfortably tied up to much more suitable people."

"I suppose you're right."

He turned the car, and they started for home again.

After a while she said regretfully:

"I'll hate parting with this car, won't you?"

"Hate it," he agreed. "I shall hate parting with every single thing I'm used to, as a matter of fact, because, as we once observed, we're the kind of people who like eating our cake and still having it."

She laughed.

"Funny we're both so calm about it."

"Not at all funny," he assured her. "We've merely made up our minds with our usual inflexibility of purpose."

"Perhaps. No one seeing us at this moment could imagine we were on the edge of a very frightening and delightful precipice. They'd take us for a prosperous young couple without a care in the world."

"Instead of what we really are." He smiled thoughtfully ahead. "A couple of adventurers, setting out on a tremendous adventure."

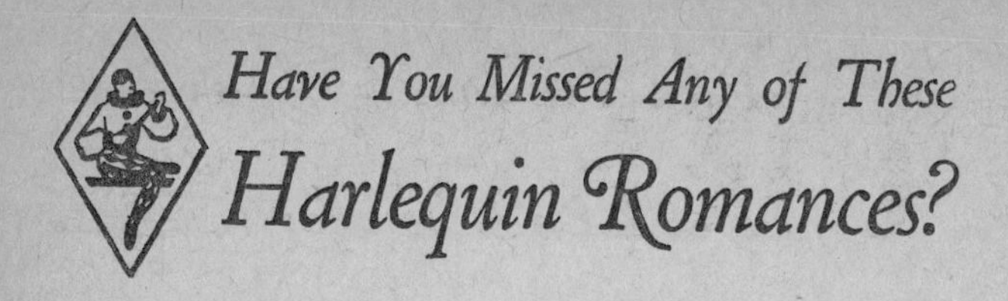
Have You Missed Any of These
Harlequin Romances?

# Have You Missed Any of These Harlequin Romances?